DEVIL'S CATCH

A Novel
by
Ernie Vecchione

CORINA BOOKS

ISBN: 978-0-9894013-0-2 (ebook)
ISBN: 978-0-9894013-1-9 (paperback)

website: www.DevilsCatch.com
blog: www.ErnieBlog.com
email: ErnieWriter@gmail.com

cover and artwork © 2013

artwork by Cintia Gonzalvez
cover design by Phillip Anderson

To everyone who had to hide a book from their parents…

Here's another one.

"The Lord will afflict you with the boils of Egypt
and with tumors, festering sores and the itch
from which you cannot be cured.
The Lord will afflict you with madness, blindness and
confusion of the mind…"

—Deuteronomy 28: 27-28

"…and if I'm lying, may the Lord strike me dead."

—Cheezburger.com

1
THE FAMILY TRIP

Elijah Wilson was hungry; there was no doubt about that. He was hungry as any twelve year old could be sitting in the back of his family's station wagon, watching the white bellies of Pocono Mountain oak trees zoom past while his parents bickered about kitchen drapes. Luckily he had stuffed his backpack with enough prepackaged snack cakes, suckers, jawbreakers and candy bars to last most normal people a decade. Sure, Elijah weighed more than the other children in his school. He had more chins than most boys his age. He even sported more pimples and blackheads on his face than his entire gym team put together. But no amount of relentless teasing and physical discomfort could ever outweigh the rich, inviting, chocolate solace of a Dingle Dog. It was barely enough to survive a weekend trip in the family's mountain cabin, for Elijah was only hungry when he was miserable.

And currently he was starving.

"Nothing but religious stations," his father grumbled. Allen Wilson was in his late forties, trim with blond hair parted in the middle and green eyes that matched his polo shirt. His impatient fingers jabbed the radio's scan button. He was a religious man, observant in all the standard Catholic rituals including mass and weekly confession—a practicing Catholic, as they all were. But they were on vacation, and if there was one area where he drew the line on vacation, it was Christian music.

The static grew louder and louder with each spin of the dial, broken only by the sporadic ranting of a backwoods preacher screaming through the speakers.

"Repent!"

Dad groaned and flicked the dial to the right.

"Redeem!" another shouted.

More static filled the car. Elijah's mother made a hairpin turn, narrowly avoiding the latest mile marker. Elijah gracefully slid the Dingle Dog from his backpack. When the radio static reached its loudest point, Elijah snapped open the plastic wrap containing the delectable chocolate tube filled with icing.

"Elijah, what was that noise?" His father's voice was a ruler-to-the-knuckles *twack* to Elijah's conscience.

"W-w-what noise?" Elijah stammered. "W-w-when?"

"Just now."

Elijah shook his head and shrugged, glad he hadn't yet taken a bite out of the delicious snack treat. His Dad would surely have seen a halo of frosting on his lips. "Nothing, why?"

"I could have sworn I heard you opening a Dingle Dog back there."

Elijah tried to hide his shock. How? How had his father heard the crinkle of two centimeters of plastic wrap when static blasted his ears from the car's tinny front speakers? And how had he known it was a Dingle Dog, of all things, and not a Crazy Cake or a Mondo Muffin or a Lemon Twistee Supreme?

"Leave the boy alone, Allen," said his mother, turning her head to wink at Elijah over her headrest. Forget the fact that she was driving, or that they were inching higher in elevation with each passing mountain mile. His mother *always* had to look people in the eye when she was talking to them. "Growing boys need their empty calories. You heard what the doctor said."

Dad rolled his eyes. "I'd be fine with his empty calories if he was growing in the right direction."

Mom wrinkled her nose and shook her head. Piled high with hairspray and stiff as a helmet, her auburn hair didn't move but she shook it anyway. As she did, the car drifted over the solid white line in the middle of the road. A giant logging truck barreled straight toward them. The trucker laid on his horn. His mother adjusted the steering wheel and strayed back into the right lane. Elijah's Dad went from scowling at his wife to scowling at the radio, blitzing through another round of static only to hear more cries of "Repent" and "Redeem," with a few "Hallelujahs" thrown in for good measure.

Elijah stared out the window. A passing tree limb scraped the window, blasting fall leaves in the car's wake. As his mother accelerated higher and higher up the mountain he wondered when he'd have the chance to take his first bite.

"Speaking of growing," his mother said, using that *I-know-we're-not-supposed-to-talk-about-the-boy-in-front-of-the-boy-but-since -he's-here-what-else-are-we-going-to-do?* tone Elijah knew too well. "Have you… you know… talked to him yet?"

"About what?" his father asked.

"You knoooow." Mrs. Wilson nudged her husband's shoulder, her hands momentarily slipping from the wheel.

Elijah licked his lips and braced for the worst. A lecture was coming. The red flush on the back of his father's neck indicated it wasn't the good kind, either.

His father sounded genuinely surprised. "What? Now?"

"Yes now," said Mrs. Wilson, peering at Elijah nervously in the rearview mirror. Another truck nearly leaped off the mountain as she drifted from lane to land and back again.

Oh God, Elijah thought to himself miserably. He cupped

his forehead in his hands and pushing his thick, black-framed glasses up his nose. *Not this talk. Not now, in an enclosed place with nowhere to hide. Or run.*

His dad cleared his throat. "Elijah, you may have noticed some changes going on in your body—"

Elijah moaned. "Dad, please. I beg of you..."

"And not just on your face, son. You may have noticed some hair...down there... in the hot spots—"

"Dad," he interrupted, "if this is about the magazines I found in your closet, I already said I'm sorry. I'm ashamed enough as it is."

"That's what we want to tell you, Elijah," his mother cooed, leaning over the headrest and peering into his eyes. "You shouldn't feel ashamed about any new feelings you might have, you know... *down there...*"

"Oh God," Elijah croaked. His stomach felt queasy, his palms sweaty, and not just because they were approaching another fifteen-mile-per hour curve going forty. He tapped his forehead against the window. The torture came fast and quick.

"And if you do have those feelings, son," added his father, "it's perfectly natural to touch yourself."

"Allen," scolded his mother. "The boy is certainly no stranger to masturbation. His sheets are practically covered with—"

"Myra!" Even his Dad thought this was too much.

Elijah broke away from the window, smeared by his

lumpy, greasy nose, and found both his parents looking at him.

"But," Elijah began, his voice cracking. "But—isn't it a sin? Nana says I'll go to hell if I keep... um, touching my hot spots."

Elijah's father winced and looked to his wife, a helpless expression on his usually domineering face. His mother blushed and, for once, paid attention to the road.

"Don't worry about what Nana says or believes. Believe in your *own* happiness, kiddo, and everything will work out fine."

Elijah frowned. It sounded good, but his father's easy advice didn't jibe with Nana's stern, daily admonitions. "But isn't it a sin to have premarital sex?"

"Only if you do it wrong." Dad chuckled, nudging his wife's ample arm.

"You're confusing him, Allen."

"He's already confused! Nana's got him afraid of his own shadow."

Elijah's mother turned toward him again and, arm hugging the passenger headrest, said, "While you're going through this phase, Elijah, you're going to feel awkward. You're going to feel inadequate. You're going to feel alone. We just want to tell you that it's all perfectly normal—"

"And," his father added, "no matter how alone you feel, there is someone meant for everyone."

"So find yourself a nice girl."

"And don't live your life in fear of punishment by some vengeful Old Testament God. Personally, I don't believe in a god who would punish you for touching yourself. And if I'm lying, may the Good Lord str—"

The windshield in front of him exploded. A pipe burst through Allen Wilson's throat, spraying his wife and son with a firehose of arterial blood.

Mom gasped, features frozen, hands white-knuckled on the steering wheel. The driver's side windshield shattered. Two PVC pipes slammed into the side of her head.

The car screeched to a violent halt.

Elijah's shoulder belt locked. His head jerked forward, coming to rest just centimeters from the pipe that had nearly decapitated his father. Blood was all over Elijah—his hair, his ears. Its scent filled his nose. He blinked and wiped his eyes.

Six or seven industrial iron pipes skewered the front seats. The windshield was replaced with the logo of the back of the delivery truck his mother had slammed into.

It read *Paul's PVC Pipe Emporium*.

Above the truck, a traffic light flashed from red to green.

Elijah sat in his seat, transfixed, unable to look away from his parents' shattered skulls. A familiar voice muttered from inside the car.

"Mom? Dad? Are we there yet?"

It was *his* voice.

Within moments, the small mountain road bustled with people. Sirens wailed in the distance. Strangers surrounded the car, beating on the windows, jiggling the handles of the back doors, trying to get in. Elijah leaned back in his seat and felt something sticky.

A Dingle Dog was squished between his fingers.

The car radio kicked in. An old hymnal creaked through the hissing speakers. Elijah recognized it as one of Nana's favorites:

> *Are you washed in the blood,*
> *In the soul-cleansing blood of the Lamb?*
> *Are your garments spotless? Are they white as snow?*
> *Are you washed in the blood of the Lamb?*

Rubbing his head absently, tears spilling like Christ's blood, Elijah peered out the spider-cracked side window to a sign across the road:

Welcome to Devil's Catch.

2
THE PLAN

CHAPTER ONE

Elijah arrived at Holy Ghost High School early, as he did every morning. He liked to have his crappy thrift store-bought bike already locked up behind the school racks before the rest of the general population showed up. He never forgot the day he rode it to school with five minutes to spare. His classmates dissolved into hilarious laughter and pointed as he wheeled it into the playground, his back tires making a farting sound all the way.

Even now, Elijah shuddered at the memory.

He unfolded his navy blazer from the milk crate basket tied to the back seat and slipped it on over his powder blue dress shirt, part of his school uniform. The jacket had a crest, something with an eagle and a dragon, which seemed more Harry Potter than Holy Ghost to Elijah, but he was sure it was in the Bible. Somewhere.

Elijah leaned against the side of the building and scanned the bike path for his friend George. Cars passed in front of the school. Some contained teachers, others contained parents. Every so often a student lucky enough to own a car drove by. He checked his watch. George was late, as usual, and why not? He didn't have to be embarrassed about *his* bike.

Elijah walked alone across the commons. The grounds were getting more crowded now, and it was a struggle to make it through the bottleneck at the front double doors.

Holy Ghost High was his home away from home and Elijah was its model student. He was quiet, did what he was told and never, ever stood out from the crowd. *Live quietly and peaceably and fearfully and God will keep you safe*, Nana always said. And Elijah always did. She was proud of him, he knew that. After his parents had died in a freak car accident six years earlier, all he had in the world was his Nana.

And George, of course.

Inside the school hall, Elijah steered toward the lockers, hoping to avoid the bigger cluster of students as they gathered in the inevitable high school cliques. He took out his homework to stow for later. Unfortunately top jock Brody Masters reached over with his ham fist and knocked the canvas bag from Elijah's hands.

Laughter erupted in the halls as the bag spilled papers, folders and textbooks all over the polished floor. Brody and his buddies laughed the loudest, ambling away in a jumble of blue blazers and thick necks.

Elijah grumbled and reached for his Sociology assignment. A pair of faintly painted fingernails snatched it before he could. He looked up, fist poised to shove back, only to blink at the angel kneeling next to him.

It wasn't an angel. Angels didn't carry backpacks. But the way the morning light filtered in through the thin window tiles along the ceiling bathed the girl's head in a solar halo.

Elijah blinked and raised a hand, blocking out the sun. The impression left was no less saintly. She was as lithe as she was slender; he could tell that from the way her stooped body seemed to fold on itself like ribbon candy that went on forever.

"Thanks," he muttered.

"Don't let the gorillas get you down," the girl said. She snatched up the last of his papers and dragged him to his feet. Her eyes were striking emerald; her long, straight hair the color of burnt amber. Her skin was so pale and paper thin it appeared she could burst into flame from the sun's rays at any moment. The whimsical expression on her face said she would probably enjoy it.

"I... I... must have lost my balance," he murmured.

"Whatever you say, tough guy." She winked and dragged him toward his locker by the hand. By *his* hand. In hers.

Elijah looked down to make sure. Yes, she was holding his hand. Still.

She was just ahead of him. Black knee-high socks hugged the top of her white calves. The backs of her thighs played hide-and-seek with her snug-waisted school-approved skirt. The skirt twirled and, too soon, she caught him looking. Seeing his surprised expression, she offered a crooked smile—cool, calm, confident.

"My name's Annie Rourke," she said.

The longer he looked at her, the safer he felt around her. She smelled of incense, not the putrid kind they used in church, but the inviting, vaguely exotic kind you might smell when you passed by the local New Age bookstore downtown—the one that sold hemp sandals and tie dyed T-shirts and organic wheat grass. Lilac or roses, maybe, and something else he couldn't quite put his finger on.

She was clearly waiting for his half of the introduction. He quickly snapped to attention.

"I'm Elijah," he managed to say without stammering. "I haven't seen you around here before."

God, did he really say that?

"I'm new," she said.

"How long have you been here?"

"A few weeks."

"Oh."

He realized they were still holding hands. Before his palm could turn clammy, he slid his hand from her grasp.

Annie looked around the bustling commons. "So, what's this place like?"

Elijah shrugged. He was nauseatingly afraid she was growing bored with him. "It's okay as long as you avoid the crowds. And the nuns."

"Just like every Catholic school then," she said, turning back from the maddening crowds to focus on him. "And you—what's your dilly-yo?"

"Dilly... yo?" he asked.

Annie nodded, eagerly, as if she was actually interested. "You know, '*deal.*' What are you into? Who do you hang with? Like, for instance, do you happen to know this giant wall of meat rapidly approaching you?"

Huh, he tried to say, but two giant hands lifted him by the shoulders and spun him around.

"Max," Elijah blurted, trying to squirm free. By the time he did, Annie Rourke had drifted away, the back of her jacket lost in a sea of Catholic blue.

"Elijah! My man!" Max shouted, jostling the much smaller junior as if he was a tackling dummy on the practice field. Max Hardesty was the starting linebacker for the Holy Ghost Harridans, the high school's football team. He was a giant of a man, if you can call a seventeen year old a *man.* But Max had enough weight, muscle, and the visible beginnings of a moustache to qualify.

What seemed strange to Elijah—what freaked him out, honestly—was that Max knew his name. As far as Elijah knew, the only way Max might know his name was if he had seen it written in permanent ink on Elijah's underwear tag when he gave him a wedgie freshman year.

"C'mere, worm," Max said, tousling Elijah's hair. "I just want to thank you for inviting me to your party this weekend. Look, I know we haven't spoken much in the past year, but this weekend is going to be the tits. The tits!"

Elijah rubbed his shoulder, already sore from Max's heavy-handed embrace. "Uh, what?"

The hall was crowded now. Max leaned in conspiratorially. His breath smelled like cigarettes and chewing gum. "I know all about how you and George are sneaking to your grandmother's cabin for the weekend. Your secret's safe with me."

Elijah's neck flushed red. His buddy George had been pestering him for weeks to use Nana's cabin in the woods so he could lose his virginity to his on-again, off-again girlfriend Felicity. Elijah had turned him down repeatedly. When did "no" suddenly mean "yes?"

Elijah made guttural noises as the blush reached his cheeks. "Cabin? Secret?"

"I'm gonna bring Gretchen, dude. I hope you're cool with that because between you and me she promised me her v-card and man, my head is gonna pop if I don't get inside of *that* before Monday morning."

Elijah could barely breathe with Max crowding him into the nearest row of lockers. "Wait, what? Gretchen? Who?"

Max scanned the crowded hallway until he spotted a petite brunette. She was walking with friends, all freshmen, all giggling, all wearing their navy blazer sleeves rolled to the elbows.

"YO, GRETCHEN!" Max bellowed across the hall.

Gretchen Podowsky heard him immediately; her cherubic, barely-legal young face lit up when she saw who had called her out.

"YOU. ME." Max then performed a series of impressively agile pelvic thrusts that could have inspired a nun to orgy. "CABIN. THIS WEEKEND."

Gretchen squealed with delight, yanked out the retainer from her mouth and nodded feverishly. "Okay."

Max grabbed Elijah and yanked him up to his side. "THANKS TO THIS GUY."

"Cool beans." Gretchen reinserted her retainer and casually walked away with her friends.

Max slapped Elijah on the shoulder. Elijah's knees buckled. "You see that, dude? She is hot for it. Man, this weekend? It's going to be the tits. The tits!"

Elijah's eyes searched for the nearest escape. Or at the very least a place to lie down. Forever. He started to move away when Max grabbed Elijah by the arm.

"Since you're the host of this thing I gotta ask you... who's bringing the condoms?"

CHAPTER TWO

"Dude, I apologize about Max," George said, opening his locker. He had wanted to tell Elijah himself, but Max had gotten to him first. "Max has been working on Gretchen all year and when I told him about us going to the cabin this weekend, he got excited. It seemed wrong not to invite him. You know... un-Christian-like. I didn't think it was a big deal."

Elijah shook his head, unimpressed. "I never said we were going."

"I thought you did," George bluffed. "Yesterday."

Elijah grimaced. "I said I'd think about it."

"You did?" George said, feigning surprise. "I must have misheard." He paused for effect. "So have you decided?"

Elijah slammed his locker shut. "The answer is no, George."

The two had been locker neighbors since freshman year. Physically they could not have been more opposite.

George Freeling, it was said, could have been a model for a Catholic Teen catalogue—so fair was his hair, so assured was his stride, so white were his teeth. Elijah, on the other hand, always seemed a few inches shorter and thirty pounds heavier than everybody else. Over the years they had bonded over comic books (Elijah's Nana forbade them in her house so George was keeper of the collection) and Bible study (Elijah was a wiz with names and places whereas George couldn't be bothered). By all rights George should have been hanging around much cooler people than Elijah Wilson, but he didn't. The truth was Elijah was his only friend. He simply didn't see the point of needing anyone else. And now his only friend was storming down the hallway, taking with him George's only chance at sleeping with the cheerleading captain of the school...

No. There was no way he would let Elijah back out now.

George raced to catch up with him. "Come on, Elijah. It's not like your grandmother's using it or anything."

Elijah muttered helplessly. "Can't you lose your virginity in your bedroom like every other guy on the planet?"

George flinched. "What, with my brother in the other room?"

"Well, what about your mother's car?" Elijah suggested. "Or a motel room?"

George clucked his tongue. "You want me to go to some fleabag motel room with Felicity when you have a whole cabin in the mountains just sitting there?"

"It's not my cabin," Elijah blurted, his voice raising an octave. "Besides, what am I going to tell my grandmother?"

"Say you're visiting me this weekend. I'll say I'm visiting you."

"That will never work."

It would, of course. Elijah just didn't want it to. Lying to his Nana was akin to crimes against humanity.

"And what am *I* supposed to do all weekend?"

"Find someone," George said. "Anyone! Your virginity isn't going to lose itself. Haven't you ever dreamed of being with someone instead of being alone? You gotta stop being afraid all the time."

"I am *not* afraid."

George saw he was getting to him. "Then how come in the years I've known you, you haven't once asked out a girl? Not once?"

Elijah's tone oozed defensiveness. "I don't know… shouldn't you wait until you're in love?"

George rolled his eyes. "Felicity and I *are* in love, Elijah."

This came as news to Elijah. "You are?"

"There are many different kinds of love, dude. There's the love for an animal. There's the love for parents. And then there's the love that I have."

"What kind is that?"

George slapped Elijah on his shoulder and said, "The kind that happens when a girl says yes to sex. Praise God."

Elijah snorted sarcastically. "I hope you the two of you have beautiful babies together."

George's cell phone bleated out the buzz of an incoming text. "That's her."

His fingers flew across his cell phone keyboard and within seconds he sent his text message and winked at Elijah. "I told her you're thinking about it."

Elijah's nostrils flared. George knew he'd said the wrong thing.

"I am not thinking about it!" Elijah insisted, face flustered. "I can't do this! All right? Can we just drop it?"

George shook his head. That was it. He hadn't wanted to do it, but Elijah had backed him into a corner.

He went for his Hail Mary pass.

George slipped his phone from his pocket and wrote Felicity a second text.

"What are you doing now?" Elijah asked.

George paused, giving his little pal one last chance to back out now. "I'm sorry, Elijah. I knew that was a shitty thing to do, inviting Max like that. You're my best friend since ninth grade. Whatever you say is cool. It was unfair for me to dump it on you like that..."

Elijah eyed him suspiciously. "Really?"

George suppressed the urge to smirk. Instead, he bit his lip and followed it with a heavy sigh. "Sure, of course, pal. I mean, Max will be disappointed, no doubt. He was looking forward to busting Gretchen's cherry, but hey, he can deal. *Feliiiciiity*, on the other hand..." He stretched out the vowels of Felicity as long as he could for emphasis. "*She's* going to have a hard time with it."

Elijah gulped. "Like... *how* hard a time?"

George frowned, making a major I'm-really-concerned-about-her-mental-health face. "Hard to tell, dude. She's not that stable to begin with. You know she's off her meds, right?"

Elijah's ears perked up. "Again?"

George shook his head grimly. "Her doctor's trying to wean her off of them. He says she should avoid stress, especially disappointment. This counts as both..."

Of course, George knew all along how Felicity would react. Felicity Cleary, captain of the cheerleading squad and social pride of her school, was, in a word, nuts. She had been a living, breathing, walking pharmacy ever since her parents divorced five years ago. On her best days, the slightest change in plans would send her into fits. On her worst? All bets were off. No sane man in his right mind would have put up with her for a minute—if he was blind. But because Felicity looked like a Sports Illustrated cover girl come to life, with toned abs, Nordic features, and strong, athletic legs on a six-foot frame, George put in the time. After months of being on the receiving end of her mood swings and gradually earning her trust, he was finally in a position where he could consummate the relationship and get rid of his virgin label once and for all.

He hit the send button. Dramatically, so that Elijah could see him do it.

The little dude's face froze.

"W-w-what...?" Elijah stammered. "What did you just send her?"

He sounded so scared George had to stifle a smile. "What'd you think, Elijah? I told her the truth. I had to break it to her somehow."

They both heard the scream—dramatic, and on cue— coming from the gym.

George hit the double gym doors first, Elijah a distant second. They found Felicity slumped under the basketball hoop, her long legs splayed out beneath her, tiny waist sobbing as she choked back tears. She was surrounded by three of her cheerleader friends. The girls practiced cheer every morning before class, even in the off-season. The nuns of the school had remarked if the girls had shown as much devotion to their faith as they had to cheer, the sisters would be out of a job.

"George!" one of the girls scolded as he approached. "What did you say to her?"

"It wasn't me," he protested, shooing them away.

Another girl leaned in and whispered to him, "You know she's off her meds again, right?"

George gave an understanding nod. "I know, I know."

The girls each took a look at Elijah, turned up their noses and peeled off in a pack, plaid skirts flashing black thong panties as they twirled away, one after the other as if it were one of their Friday night routines.

Felicity gazed up at George, her pretty face marred by desperation and desire, her giant pleading eyes locked on his. "You don't know how much I needed this weekend, George. You don't know the pressure I'm under. The stress of coming up with routines. The rhymes..."

George lifted Felicity off the floor and held her, burying his face in her hair. It smelled of her fancy perfume. He had never told her it made her smell like Christmas fruitcake and mothballs. He brushed a long blonde lock of hair out of her face and then swiped her running mascara away with one thumb. "It's okay, honey. We can do it some other time—"

She shoved him away and punched him in the chest, hard, knocking the wind out of him. He doubled over and gasped for air. It felt like being hit by a bowling ball.

"YOU HAVE NO IDEA!" Felicity shouted. "*YOU* try figuring out words that rhyme with Holy Ghost. Just try it!"

"I know, honey, I know," George gasped, his lungs

filling with air once again. He shot a look to Elijah. He needed to set the hook, and deep. "Go on. Tell her, Elijah."

If eyeballs could whimper, Elijah's certainly would have at that moment. Elijah took a step forward, uncertain. George used his hand to make a come on, come on gesture.

"Look," Elijah muttered, "Felicity, it's not really my decision..."

George watched Felicity cross her arms, which pushed out her chest. A long, thin dangle of snot hung from the tip of her button nose, but not even that could distract him from the brilliance that was her bosom. God, he needed this weekend.

"I know," Felicity whispered, her throat dry from crying. She swiped at her eyes, blurring the mascara even more. The snot remained untouched. "I'm just being selfish.... *Like everyone says...*"

"No, no," Elijah said, taking another step forward. "I mean, I just... it's not... well..."

George held his breath. This was it. Do or die time. He had tried everything so far to close the deal. The pleading, the prodding, the gentle nudging, the letting-it-slip-to-Max. Elijah might be able to say no to him, but to a weeping, whimpering six-foot girl?

"I guess..." Elijah teetered. "I suppose it's no big deal."

Magically, Felicity stopped sobbing.

"Really?" she squealed, clenching her fists, shoving them under her chin, blinking those beautiful blue eyes, and then extending her arms. George prepared for the embrace of all embraces, but she blew past him and engulfed Elijah—little fat Elijah—wrapping her arms around him and practically smothering his face in her chest.

"You and I are going to be *best* friends," Felicity gushed and, in another display of her amazing strength, she plucked Elijah up off the waxed gym floor and swung him in the air like a kindergartener on the playground.

George shook his head. Manipulating Elijah was easy. In fact, it was too easy. Elijah just wore his too-big heart on his too-big sleeve, that's all. But truth be told, his wide-eyed ignorance about the real world had raked George's patience long ago. It wasn't always easy being friends with a guy like Elijah, but George wasn't exactly Mr. Popularity either.

All that would change after a weekend alone in Elijah's cabin, he reminded himself.

CHAPTER THREE

Elijah slumped onto his favorite seat at the far back library table, exhausted from the mental drama he experienced that morning at the hands of George and his Amazon girlfriend, Felicity. He had started out strong, stood firm in the face of all George's arguments and ploys, but they had chipped away every ounce of resolve until he'd done what he promised himself he wouldn't do: give in. He'd been defeated, played. Now he was stuck with a bunch of clods at his grandmother's cabin, where they would christen every piece of furniture with their sexual libidos while he cringed, plugging his ears and clutching his knees to his chest, all the while praying to God for forgiveness for being such a pathetic jellyfish.

How had he gotten himself into this? His stomach lurched. He was supposed to be at B-Lunch, but the thought of watching George gloat and do crazy, acrobatic, tribal handshakes with Max over their double orders of macaroni and cheese made him nauseous.

What if George was right? George was a jock and a meathead and a lousy friend at times, but he was still a friend. He'd never lied to Elijah before. Maybe he was telling the truth when he said that Felicity was *the one*. And hadn't Elijah's father, all those years ago, said that sex wasn't wrong if it was with the one you loved? Maybe sex wasn't the worst sin in the world. Maybe God didn't frown upon it like Nana said.

Maybe everything would turn out all right.

Two girls at the next table gossiped loudly. Their blather, interspersed with the occasional "I know, right?" and "Soooo lame," along with the texting frenzy of clicking nails on cell phones had been background noise ever since Elijah walked in and found his chair.

"Did you hear about the sex party this weekend?" asked the first girl with the louder fingernails.

"Were you invited?" asked her friend scrolling through her email messages.

"Not yet," chirped the first confidently, "but I hear *everyone's* going."

Elijah's head hit the table with a loud thud, which might have explained why he didn't hear the chair on the other side of the table slide out.

"Stressed out, huh?" came a vaguely familiar, feminine voice.

Elijah glanced up to find the new girl, Annie, sitting

opposite him. Her hair was pulled back; her face looked oddly round without her rich red strands falling around it.

He groaned and let his head slump back to the table, eliciting a chuckle from Annie. She sounded a little like a chirping bird.

"I guess I would be, too," she said, "if I was hosting a weekend sex party."

Elijah sat back up. "How did you—"

Annie jerked a thumb at the two girls behind Elijah. "Same way they did. It's all over the school."

She made a show of looking him up and down, her green eyes squinting with scrutiny.

His insides did a belly flop.

"Funny, you don't strike me as some big swinger."

"I'm not," he rushed to say.

She nodded knowingly and looked over her shoulder at the librarian, Mrs. Thrush, who sat reading her monthly romance novel. With the librarian otherwise occupied, Annie tore open a package of granola bars and handed him one. Elijah took it gratefully, but waited until she took her first bite to do the same.

"Thanksh," he said around a crumbly mouthful.

"So tell me," she asked around her own mouthful, "how does one host a sex party?"

"I don't know," he shrugged. "It's my first time. And I'm not even the one getting lucky."

Annie paused, thick eyebrows arched. "You're not

bringing anyone? What are you going to do while everyone else at the party is shagging?"

Elijah frowned and swallowed the last of his granola bar. "Dunno. Sing Kumbayah by the fireplace while everyone upstairs is doing it, I guess." He realized he was talking to a perfect stranger on the subject of sex. He sat up in his chair and straightened his tie, thinking that would excuse all the raunch. "Sorry about all this... talk."

Annie smiled, tapping Elijah's shoe with hers. "You mean sex? I'm not offended about sex."

She leaned in close to Elijah, their faces nearly touching.

"Between you and me," she whispered conspiratorially, her breath warm and cinnamon and raisin-scented from her granola bar, "I know some people who have had sex, and I suspect a few of them are in this room."

Elijah grinned as he realized she was having fun at his expense. Still, her crooked smile and the closeness of her breath as it spilled against his chin were intoxicating.

Pointing around the room, still whispering, still leaning close, Annie said, "That couple over there? See how she puts her chest on the table when she leans over to talk to him? They've had sex. That girl staring out the window? See that faraway look? Had it. That boy over there? See how he walks? He's had it and he's thinking about having it again."

Elijah enjoyed her sense of humor, and the fact that he could see the swell of her breasts inside her snug uniform shirt didn't hurt things, either. She started to pull away but he pointed at a random girl in the library stacks, leaning up on uncomfortable shoes to reach a book on the top shelf.

"And her?" he asked, playing along.

"Oh, she probably had sex this morning."

He covered his mouth to stifle a laugh. "And that guy?" he asked, nodding toward a stocky boy in the paperback section.

"For sure, he's getting ready to meet someone for sex right now."

He pointed to the janitor.

She nodded enthusiastically, their foreheads almost touching and mouthed, "Sex. All day and all night."

"How about them?" Elijah asked about the two girls still gossiping and texting at the next table.

Annie's lips drew his focus. "Sex, sex and more sex."

"And the librarian?" he asked.

Annie snorted, shaking her head. "No, she reads romance novels. She hasn't had sex in a looong time."

They giggled, and she pulled back, almost... reluctantly. Or maybe it was just him.

"See?" she said. "Sex isn't such a bad thing. After all, that's how we got here. On some wonderful night, some guy railed our mothers."

Elijah stifled a laugh, then composed himself. "That's what everybody thinks—that I think sex is bad. But I don't.

I just believe you should be in love first."

"Who says they aren't? All those friends coming over this weekend, I mean?"

He exhaled dryly. "You don't know them. The only thing they love is themselves. That, and feeling good."

"Is that so bad?" she asked. Her voice was soft, not challenging, just... curious. He wasn't used to that. The only other person he talked to on the regular—George—was either bellowing or bragging or bullying, if he was talking to Elijah at all.

"No, but... it'd be nice to think of others. Isn't that what love is?"

He couldn't believe he was here, having this discussion with her. New girls caught on pretty quickly that Elijah wasn't exactly Big Man on Campus and, if they had somehow talked to him before they found out, they rarely ever did again. But Annie seemed different. She had already seen him humiliated, rescued him and was still sticking around? Was something wrong with her?

Or, he considered with wonder and awe, was there something *right* with him?

Annie gently nudged his foot, startling him back to the conversation. Her expression said *Hello? Are you listening?*

"I'm sorry... what?"

"Did you already say yes?"

"To what? The sexscapade party? Yeah, unfortunately, I did."

"Bummer," she said, chewing her lip. "Can't go back on your word now. You'll lose your friends."

"Friends?" he blurted, more loudly than he meant to. Then, softer, "That might not be such a bad thing."

She laughed, low and throaty.

He fiddled with the pencil in his hand. She toyed with the necklace around her throat: a crucifix necklace. They both fondled their objects, turning them over and back again nervously, without thinking. He stared at the crucifix, then his eyes drifted to her neck, pale and pink above a high stiff white collar. The pause stretched beyond awkward, but she seemed to be enjoying it.

Elijah, to his surprise, enjoyed it as well.

The bell rang. The girls at the next table and the kids in the stacks whose sexual escapades they had guessed at all headed for the door, but Elijah and Annie just sat there. For his part, Elijah was scared to move, as if the very act of standing would break the moment's magical spell.

Finally she sighed and said, "I guess you'll just have to suffer alone."

"I guess so," he croaked, watching her stand.

She bent over to gather her things. Her crucifix dangled in mid-air casting a slight shadow upon her chest.

The words *spiritual fruits* came to mind.

A young couple stood at the reception desk, checking books out. As she walked by, Annie pointed playfully at their backs and mouthed the word, "Sex."

Later when he replayed their conversation in his head, stopping to enjoy and savor several key moments, Elijah swore there was something—a smile, a gesture, a tone perhaps— that sounded vaguely like an invitation.

Of course, he was probably imagining it.

CHAPTER FOUR

Elijah was afraid to clip too far. He just wasn't sure where the fungus ended and Nana's toe began.

"Make sure to cut them straight across now, dear," Nana mumbled through a mouth full of chewed popcorn. "Otherwise I'll get ingrown toenails."

Elijah made no comment, only nodded. It wasn't as if she could see over her huge stomach, or bend down to reach her toes herself, which was why he had been called into nail-clipping duty in the first place. This was how he spent all his Friday nights. Thursdays were for ear inspection. On Saturdays, the lotion came out for varicose vein rubs.

Nana was propped up on several pillows, lounging in her king-sized bed under a black velvet picture of Jesus shaking Elvis's hand. She lay large and dowdy in a flowing pink and orange housedress, her favorite teal Tupperware bowl full of dollar store microwave popcorn resting on her ample lap. She seldom left the house, even for church, and limited her worship to sending money to televangelists.

But tonight the TV flickered and screamed—and screamed and screamed. On the screen, the comely young co-ed smiled to think she had escaped the killer. A machete severed the door of the locker she was hiding in and slid between her breasts. Red arterial blood spewed like the Devil's garden hose.

"You know," Elijah said idly, "it disturbs me when you watch the Scream Channel."

"Why?" Nana asked, her hand full of popcorn pausing on the way to her mouth.

"All these horror movies... they're not good for you. They're... gross."

Nana chomped the corn and swallowed. "Some call them horror. I call them *Christian*. Where else but in these movies can you find the confirmation that God exists? Sinners sin. Get punished. God reigns. Cue credits."

She smiled, proud of her philosophy, one eye on him, one eye on the screen as she pointed a gnarled, greasy finger and said, "Look!"

Despite himself, Elijah obeyed. There, on the screen, beneath the world's largest crucifix, a teen boy had the top of his head sliced clean off with a machete. His brain jiggled like a Jell-O mold on the top of his exposed skull.

Elijah's eyes avoided the screen and drifted to Nana's

wall art. The cheap wood paneling was covered in more crucifixes and apostle faces than a missionary gift shop. A black velvet DaVinci Last Supper hung above a plastic glow-in-the-dark Madonna and Child. Scattered among all the Jesus memorabilia were framed snapshots of Elijah's and Nana's life together: Elijah sitting before a birthday cake in the shape of a cross, Elijah attending his first Catechism class, Elijah wearing a suit two sizes too small on the day of his confirmation. If he looked glum in all of those pictures, it wasn't Nana's fault. She left her mountain cabin to buy the tiny, plain, severe house at the end of a street they now called home. Whatever her shortcomings, she did her best. It was just ever since the accident Elijah felt like he was living someone else's life.

Unfortunately, it was *his*.

Elijah clipped another toe. He held his breath at the gassy, slightly moldy smell that wafted from the fresh clip. He hoped George appreciated what he had to endure to get Nana to agree to his weekend getaway.

"You sure you want to spend all weekend at George's house?" Nana asked. "Can't he just come here? I could make my special corn chip casserole."

"Oh, that would be awesome, Nana. You know how George loves your casseroles, but... see... we're doing a project, and it's on his computer and, since you believe the internet is where the Devil lurks, well, we can only do it over there."

41

"You'll thank me one day when your soul is saved, Elijah," she said, setting her bowl aside and licking her fingers clean.

As Elijah clipped her last nail and settled in for a good buffing, Nana eyed him suspiciously. "You're not thinking of going to the cabin in Devil's Catch, are you Elijah?"

Elijah's hand froze in the middle of sanding down one of Nana's rock hard toenails. "No... why? What makes you say that? I mean, I've forgotten all about that place."

Nana's double chins glistened in the television's blue glow. "Good. There's a good reason we haven't gone up there, besides the accident. You see, Devil's Catch is a special place..."

Her voice grew wistful. She stared out the moonlit window next to her bed as she continued, "So high up on the mountains you can practically touch God's face. If you were to be up to mischief there, you'd be sure to catch the Devil."

"I guess that's why you call it Devil's Catch, hah?"

If Nana heard his feeble attempt at a joke, she didn't answer. She continued to peer out the window instead, as if she had forgotten he was in the room.

Elijah's throat constricted in a sharp throb. He wondered if one of Nana's toenails had found its way past his open lips when he clipped it. He buffed the last toe with an Emory board when she finally turned to him, her face impassive and impossible to read.

"You can go to George's."

Elijah stifled a yelp. "Really?"

"Yes," she nodded, picking up her bowl full of unpopped kernels. "The moon will be full this weekend. That means God will be keeping His eye on you and keep you out of mischief. Besides, there's a Friday the 13th marathon this weekend and I don't want to be distracted."

Elijah exhaled a sigh of relief. He gathered up the clippers, the clippings, the bowl of soapy water and the Emory board and stood.

"Thanks, Nana." He could barely hide his enthusiasm.

"And Elijah... always remember..."

She pulled him close to her on the bed and poked her finger into his chest.

"God has His finger on your heart."

Elijah considered about calling George to give him the good news but thought better of it. Let him have one more sleepless night before giving him the go-ahead in the morning. It was the least Elijah could do to repay the psychological torture George had inflicted on him for the past two weeks.

He sat on his bed beneath a poster of Jim Caviezel in bloody agony from Elijah's favorite movie, *The Passion of the Christ*. The room was small and cramped. A crooked bookshelf in the corner featured all of the Left Behind books, spines cracked, passages highlighted and pages dog-eared from multiple readings.

Outside his window, the mostly full moon sat, squat and fat, over the city of Haddonfield.

Elijah heard something crinkle as he got comfortable. Beneath the quilt, he found the latest issue of the Holy Ghost High Hornet, his school's student newspaper. Featured on the cover was the "New Girl of the Month," Annie Rourke.

He eased back onto his pillows. The moon was so bright, he didn't bother with the lamp on his nightstand. He stared at the picture, black and white but taking up nearly one quarter of the front page. Annie stood near the oak in the commons area, long legs crossed at her ankles. She leaned one hand against the giant trunk and posed, shyly, for the school photographer. A caption under the picture read: "New girl Annie Rourke takes a break between classes to enjoy nature and reflect on life at Holy Ghost High."

It wasn't the greatest picture, he had to admit. Where she had been so confident and flip in the library earlier that week, flashing that cocky, crooked smile and batting those giant green eyes, here she looked clenched and uncomfortable, as if she already knew what all the other girls at school would say about her the minute it hit the stands. She looked a little... lost.

That was something he could readily identify with.

Elijah remembered the way her fingers toyed with the

silver crucifix around her long, slender neck. He smelled her, still, that vaguely intoxicating scent of vanilla and incense and cool, clean bath water.

He gulped then looked up, as if Nana might have somehow wandered unnoticed into his room. His eyes fell on the framed photo of his parents on his nightstand. It was a studio portrait, the same one they took every few years. Just the three of them. Dad wore a maroon sports coat and gold tie. Mom was in her Sunday best, white ruffles around her collar, plump arms resting on the back of a chair.

Elijah smiled wistfully to see their faces staring back at him... then guiltily as he noticed the erection pushing against his boxer shorts.

He shoved the picture face down onto the bedside table then returned to gazing at Annie and her wide, mysterious eyes. His free hand crept steadily toward the waistline of his—

BAAM!

Elijah jumped.

The noise had come from outside his window.

He stood up abruptly, reaching for a pillow to cover his bulging manhood as he stumbled toward the windowsill.

Outside the moon seemed to be shining even more brightly. The sidewalk in the alley was empty. No prowlers, no burglars, no Peeping Toms, not even George stumbling around in the trash bins hoping to get early word on whether or not their sinful weekend was a go.

Elijah turned back to bed, literally scratching his head, when the window shattered behind him. He spun around in time to see the jagged edge of a PVC pipe stop just shy of his nose.

He blinked—

And found himself lying in bed, the sheets twisted around his ankles, his forehead covered in perspiration.

Elijah sat up, gasping for air, his heart pounding. The window remained intact. He reached for the lamp on the nightstand.

A cold, ghostly hand grabbed his elbow.

Elijah screamed and found himself staring up into the face of his father, Allen Wilson.

"Dad?"

His father's face came into focus. It was as lifelike and lively as the day he'd last seen him. And yet, blood oozed from the jagged holes left behind by the PVC pipes all those years ago. Through his torn windpipe, Allen Wilson croaked, "Remember, son, to believe in your own happiness."

"And don't forget," came a voice to his right. Elijah was startled to see his mother Myra sitting beside him. Half of her head was gone. Brain fluid oozed over her eyelids. She looked down at the crusty semen-stained bedspread and frowned. "Keep your sheets clean."

Elijah closed his eyes and moaned. When he opened

them again, his parents were gone. The room was empty and the sun had risen high enough over the neighbor's roof for its rays to land squarely on the crucifix above his head.

It had only been a dream within a dream, a nightmare within a nightmare.

Or it was a message. A message from God.

If only he was smart enough to figure out what the message was.

Thinking, thinking now... God didn't want him to go to Devil's Catch. It was too dangerous for him and his friends. Yes, that had to be it. But why use his parents? Keep your sheets clean. That had to have been a clue... about what exactly? Dirty sheets meant something. Lustful thoughts. Thoughts of sex. Sex was bad and had to abstained from at all cost... Got it.

Whew. He had broken the code. All praise to God, who made him.

Elijah looked at the clock. It was 7 a.m. It wasn't too late. He would call George and make up an excuse, any excuse. He was used to disappointing George. He was good at faking sickness. That was it. If he called him right now and pretended to be sick, it would give George time to let everyone else know. Sure, they'd be mad at him come Monday. They'd harass him in gym or at lunch or both... but how different was that from every other day? It would just be more of the same, wouldn't it? Being the target of anger was better than being ignored all the time, right? He'd take the coward's way out, Elijah decided, and happily. Fearfully made, that's how God made him after all...

The door flew open. Elijah's heart pounded again as he saw his Nana standing there in her fuzzy slippers and baggy bathrobe.

"Wake up, Elijah," she flustered, waving an egg-covered spatula in her hand. "Your friends are here."

3
THE CABIN

CHAPTER ONE

Felicity drew herself away from primping in the rear view mirror just in time to avoid barreling into a tree.

"Babe," George shrieked as he peeled his long fingers away from his baby blue eyes. "Cool it with the makeup, okay?"

"'*Cool it with the makeup,*'" she mimicked in a nasally voice. "Are you new here? There will be *no* cooling it with the makeup."

In the rear view mirror, Gretchen looked ashen. Her shoulders were wedged between Max's and Elijah's in the backseat. "Girlfriend, am I right? Makeup trumps all?"

"Not if we all plunge off a cliff while you're sliding on lip gloss," Gretchen lisped through her heavy retainer. She smiled weakly, almost apologetically, as Felicity returned her attention to the road.

George reached over and slid a hand onto Felicity's thigh. "See, babe?" he said, pressing firmly. "Everyone agrees. You can put on all the makeup you want once we get to the cabin."

Ah yes. Sweet, safe, dependable George. The summer romance that had extended into the school year. Everyone loved him. Her friends, her parents, her psychiatrists. They all said he was "good for her." When she needed someone to lean on, George was there. The 2 a.m. phone calls when she had lost her medication? He was there. The time she threw chips at him during a party? He laughed it off. The time she stopped a cheer in the middle of a game to personally berate him for not giving her a proper birthday gift? He told her he was flattered. She had put him through hell, as she tended to do with all the people in her life, and he was still there. Yes, she'd give George what he was looking for, and make it memorable, but mostly this trip was about closure.

More exactly, it was about Max. Her ex. They had dated on and off the previous spring. God, he looked so gorgeous on the football field; those shoulders, that winner's smile. She was captain of the cheerleading team; they practically *belonged* together. She had even imagined sharing a life with him, complete with little Max babies. So when George invited Max to tag along for the weekend, everyone said how wonderful it was of her to show the world she was strong enough and mature enough to not let Max flirting with that freshman pipsqueak in the backseat frigging bother her.

Yeah, right.

Felicity pressed her foot on the gas and watched the dials of her sweet sixteen BMW hit the red. She loved it when they went to the red. The Beamer shot up the sloped mountain road like a rocket.

Slow down now, interrupted a voice inside her head. *Pay attention to the road.*

Chastised once again, she relaxed her foot and, in payback, cranked the radio volume all the way up. She needed music to drown out the voices inside her head. The ones that said she was ugly and stupid and no one liked her and no one ever would.

From the backseat, Elijah mumbled, "Uh, Felicity, could you turn that down a smidge?"

Felicity glared back at him in the rear view mirror. His eyes were closed and he looked paler than usual. If she didn't know any better she'd have sworn he was hyperventilating.

"Yeah," echoed Max, the more handsome, more masculine version of George. "The speaker is basically right in my ear."

"Fine. Sheesh," Felicity sighed, switching off the radio altogether before looking up and swerving to avoid a car in her lane. Or maybe she was in *its* lane. Same diff. She couldn't wait to get off this crazy mountain road and into the bottle of whip cream flavored vodka she had stashed in her go bag. "I thought this was supposed to be some kind of party, right?"

"Yeah, guys," George said, copping another feel as he reached over and put the music back on but only half as loud. "Lighten up."

Felicity couldn't. And didn't. She looked at George. He was handsome enough, she supposed, though a little bland for her taste, but she never kissed with her eyes open anyway so what did it matter if her boyfriend was a giant bore? By the time she got back to school Monday morning all anyone would be talking about was her sex-romp weekend-of-sin anyway, so the four minutes of George grunting and moaning on top of her would be well worth it. Even if she had to endure it twice.

Felicity took another hairpin turn at sixty miles per hour. Her temperature rose. The voices always made her body boil. "Where is this place anyway, this... Devil's *Cat* or something?"

"Just a few more miles," Elijah promised from the back.

"You said that a few miles ago." She threw her eyes at George to indicate she needed his back-up. Like a good boy, he picked up his cue.

"Yeah, Elijah," he scoffed. "What gives?"

Elijah shook his head and stared out the window.

Max's phone vibrated. In the mirror Felicity saw him read his phone and glance over to Gretchen next to him, smiling.

That little tramp was texting Max in the car. In *her* car!

Max texted back. Gretchen waited patiently. When it was her phone's turn to buzz she eagerly read his message and giggled playfully. God, she looked so gullible and stupid back there. Supposedly she was a virgin, but the way she was dressed—super short black skirt, maroon bra and white men's shirt buttoned down to her navel and tied in a knot above her waist—could have fooled anybody.

A truck blared its horn. Felicity swerved back into her lane, narrowly avoiding being plowed off the tiny mountain road. She adjusted her steering and looked at the pale faces of her three passengers in the back.

"Phew, that was close," she exclaimed. "Can you believe these crazy drivers?"

George turned around in his seat to the group, as if she wasn't there in the car beside him. "Don't worry, gang. She took her meds." He gently placed his hand on her shoulder and whispered, "You *did* take your meds, right?"

She hated all the stupid concern over what she talking and how often. "Yes, George. I'm all set for the next forty-eight hours. Like I told you. Can everyone just please—?"

"Here," said Elijah.

"What's that now?"

Elijah pointed to the road. His face was red and spastic and he was spitting out his words, gasping for air. "Take… this… exit…."

"Okay, okay," Felicity said. She yanked the wheel and flew off the two-lane highway onto a rutted side road at a brisk fifty miles per hour. They barely avoided hitting the sign beyond the exit, a crooked, rusted old thing that read, "WELCOME TO DEVIL'S CATCH."

"Oh, this place is called Devil's *Catch*," she said. "Why didn't anyone tell me?"

Two withered crosses skewered the ground next to the sign. In the rear view, Felicity caught Elijah staring at the passing sign, his eyes glassy and solemn.

Back on the road, crude billboards demanded her attention. "IT IS TIME FOR JESUS CHRIST. LISTEN TO HIM!" read one. "WHERE WILL YOU BE IN THE RAPTURE?" read another. A third said: "PERFECT LOVE IS THE WAY TO JESUS."

Felicity wrinkled her nose and looked at George, who looked equally baffled. "Are we in Amish country?"

"A lot of religious groups went to the mountains during the Depression," Elijah volunteered. "Many believed the end of the world was coming."

Gretchen took out her retainer and slid it into a U-shaped yellow box. "And when it didn't, what happened?"

"They opened ski lodges," George joked.

"Really?" Gretchen asked, and Felicity had to flash her a look in the rear view to see if she was being serious or not; she was.

"Uh... no." George answered.

"People just forgot about this place," Elijah continued.

"Everyone except your Nana," George said.

"Praise God," Max added, sarcastically.

Felicity studied Max in the mirror, trying to detect what his sarcasm was really about—whether it was about the weekend or something about Gretchen he was trying to convey to Felicity in code—when a giant, fur-based thing appeared in the middle of the road.

"What the—?" Felicity barked, slamming on the brakes. The bald tires of her Beamer screeched. Smoke swirled around the windows as everyone in the back was propelled forward.

"What the fuck is *that*?" Felicity screamed, pointing a trembling finger at the front windshield.

The creature was bent over the carcass of some poor raccoon that had painted the asphalt with its guts and intestines. The creature glanced up at the car, pulled its lips back and snarled.

George put a reassuring hand on her shoulder. "It's a wolf, hon. It's okay. We're safe in here."

"Tell that to the wolf!"

Felicity heard the voices assemble inside her head again, throbbing and hoarse-throated. *See that wolf?* they said. *See it there? It's in your way; it's taunting you. Calling you out. You gonna let that wolf do that to you? It's kill or be killed out here, Felicity. It's you... or the wolf!*

She blinked the voices away, but her blood still boiled.

"The hell," Felicity spat, honking the horn twice then a

third time. "Hey wolf! Hey you! Fuck you!"

The wolf stood there, chewing lazily, its fur on end, its eyes dark and yellow. It soon grew bored with its meal and lumbered away, not before brushing the side of Felicity's door, its shoulders so high she could see the top of its ears as it bristled past. The wolf then leapt into the woods, disappearing in an instant.

Her heart racing and brow sweaty, Felicity imagined the wolf breaking into the cabin in the middle of the night and taking away Gretchen in its giant sized teeth, her screams echoing in the forest as she consoled a tearful Max.

The thought relaxed her immediately.

CHAPTER TWO

Elijah would have sold his soul for a Dingle Dog right then and there in the backseat, he swore it. Instead, he took a second antacid from his pocket and chewed it diligently, hoping it would untangle the knots in his stomach as Felicity steered them through the final mountain pass.

The main road to Devil's Catch was a gravel drive that wound as far as the eye could see up the mountain. Rocks spit out from beneath the car's tires. Felicity slowed the car to a crawl at the road's nearly forty-five degree angle.

One last crooked billboard awaited. Its faded letters, spiked in place decades ago and neglected since, read "REPENT! THE END IS NIGH." Someone had graffiti-ed "FUCKING" above "NIGH."

"Sweet," said Gretchen. She took her cell phone out of her pocket and snapped a picture—and pouted. "It's not sending."

Elijah faced the window, admiring the greenery.

"There's no signal up here." Under his breath he added, "Thank God." He had winced each time Gretchen and Max texted each other, even though she was practically sitting on Max's lap. At least he wouldn't have to worry about them texting each other across the breakfast table each morning.

They rounded the corner and the dense forest gave way to a natural clearing. A glistening lake dappled in the afternoon sun. Elijah spotted the quaint log cabin nestled on the edge of the woods. Behind it was a rotting farmhouse: smashed windows, sagging roof, knee-high grass. Wild flowers had sprouted here and there, displaying a smattering of purple, white and pink.

"Not *too* gothic," Gretchen said, leaning over Elijah to snap another picture.

Max leaned over and swatted Elijah's shoulder with his giant hand. "I guess you gave the gardener the decade off, huh, pal?"

"Nana hasn't taken me up here in years," Elijah answered, absently, as if to himself. "Not since..." His voice trailed, choked with emotion.

They parked a few feet away from the front porch, a ramshackle, sprawling affair that featured a cluster of rocking chairs and little wooden side tables to match. Elijah vaguely recalled sitting there on summer evenings, citronella candles lit to keep the critters away, sipping the glass of cider Nana would have put up that same day. He had so dreaded going each time; he remembered he raised such a fuss because he wasn't allowed to bring his comic books or any of the toys with which he found escape. The only entertainment he found amounted to his Bible, his thoughts of God, and the sound of crickets.

Elijah blinked; the rest of the group had already gotten out of the car. They were stretching their legs, craning their necks, arching their backs and yawning, fully engaged in the lazy and awkward dance of shaking out the side-effects of three hours in a car. He got out but did not join them; his stomach was so tied in knots he could barely stand up straight.

A Dingle Dog would have cured it, he mourned.

Felicity, to no one's surprise, was the first to bound up the front stoop and yank on the rusty brass doorknob. She was also the first to complain. "It's locked."

George sidled up behind her, placing both hands on her hips. "Of course it's locked, ninny," he breathed into her ear. "It's been shut up tight for years."

Felicity brushed his hands away. "But I gotta go to the bathroom."

A female voice from the side of the house chimed in, "You and me both."

Elijah felt his stomach untie itself. "You made it," he exclaimed.

"I said I would, right?" Radiant in black jeans and a red pullover with a high collar, Annie slid the backpack off her shoulder and addressed Felicity, who eyed her suspiciously. "I could have gone into the woods, but you never know what's behind you. I'm kinda skittish that way. I like to know where the stream is going."

Felicity was having none of it. "Who the fuck are you?" she asked, arms crossed under a heaving chest.

"I'm Annie Rourke," she said, simply. She extended her hand. When Felicity ignored the gesture with a stink-eye and a huff, Annie smiled and shook hands with the arid nothingness.

Elijah was surprised to hear himself snort. He was also surprised to realize he had completely abandoned all thoughts of Dingle Dogs.

"Who invited you?" Felicity barked.

Annie jerked a thumb proudly in Elijah's direction. "He did," she explained with a knowing smile. "It was very last minute."

Felicity was still miffed. "Well, someone could have warned us."

"I'm sorry," said Annie. One bold step toward Felicity marked her as Elijah's forever kind of heroine. "Did you buy the cabin from Elijah on your way up here, because last I checked, it was his."

As Felicity's face silently turned beet red, Elijah slid between the two girls.

"Were the directions okay?" he asked Annie.

"Fine. I made it here in no time. I even got to see a

wolf."

Elijah searched his pants pockets for the key. A sharp tinge of alarm wiggled up his spine. The group's panicked expressions became his as he dug his hand deeper into his pockets.

Then he remembered. Front shirt pocket.

The group collectively exhaled.

Elijah slid the key into the lock. It took some effort, not having been opened for so many years. The knob finally turned, but the door was stuck. He threw some muscle into it, what little of it he had. He explained, "You have to give it a push..." when the door opened and Elijah stumbled inside.

The cabin smelled of must and mold and dried moth wings but it looked exactly as he remembered it. He could see his parents, laughing and smiling as they played Scrabble on the coffee table, and Nana knitting in her favorite rocking chair by the sliding glass doors that overlooked nature's backyard. He could smell bacon and eggs wafting from the small kitchen with its cozy breakfast nook, intermingled with the always-present scent of firewood stacked neatly by the giant stone hearth. The journey may have been the stuff of nightmares, but to feel those memories again more than made up for it.

Max's voice, loud and guttural, ripped through his family reverie. "So," he asked in all seriousness, "where do I dock my tunes?"

Elijah blinked twice. "Huh?"

Max slid up to him, leaning in so close Elijah could smell the beef jerky on his breath, and whispered, "Dude, I queued up the perfect horn-dog playlist for this cherry-poppin' weekend, dog. I *need* a place to dock my tunes. How else am I gonna get Gretchen in the mood otherwise?"

Elijah pointed to the corner next to the fireplace. "Well," he suggested, "there's always this..."

It may have looked like a squat, wooden refrigerator to the others, but to Elijah, it was a long lost friend—Nana's radio console. He couldn't count how many evenings he spent sitting cross-legged at the altar of this boxy cathedral, staring at the Art Deco paneling, tracing the mesh scrim and its spider web-like design with his fingers. There were no stations up there to pick up besides religious stations, but on occasion, Elijah would hear a snippet from a vaudeville routine or the end of a radio drama, sounds so foreign to him they could have been coming from another dimension. Now he eagerly flicked the central dial and watched the old behemoth rise from the dead: inner tubes sparked to life, the station display glowed red, as did its tuning eye, or *magic* eye, as Nana called it. It was a beautiful central bulb that shimmered whenever the radio latched onto a strong signal. Over time, the eye lost its crimson luster and had decayed to a dull pink. But even now, after all those years, Elijah saw it had lost none of its eeriness.

Static hissed quietly at first, replaced by the first crackles of sound—horns and clarinets—as ballroom music from a 1930s radio program permeated the cabin.

Gretchen rolled her eyes and cooed sarcastically, "Oh yeah, this is much better."

Elijah shot her a withering glare, but she didn't catch it. She only had eyes for Max, who winked at her before bounding up the wooden stairs where the two small bedrooms waited.

"I call dibs on the master bedroom," Max cried. George was close on his tail.

Elijah frowned and followed them up, calling out with each step, "There are two bedrooms upstairs, but—"

At the top of the stairs he saw George pass Max and fling the door to the first bedroom open.

"Mine!" George called out, looking back at Max triumphantly. Max shrugged. Together they looked inside.

A single hammock hung in the corner by a dusty window overlooking the crowded tree line.

George looked at Elijah helplessly, as if he'd just found out there was no Santa Claus and, yes, his parents actually hid all those Easter eggs. "Dude, where's the bed?"

"I told you, there was only ever the sofa downstairs, this room, and—"

"My room!" Max yelled, completing his sentence, as he threw open the door to the second bedroom and raced inside, George and Elijah hot on his heels.

The musty smell was even thicker in this room. Dust mites scattered through the rays of sun streaming between the window slats. On the one side there was a tall, thin nightstand and on the other, a rocking chair. A single bed was shoved against the wall. A black field mouse sat on top of it, grooming its genitals. Sensing it had been caught, the mouse scampered onto the floor for parts unknown.

Smiling broadly, George slapped Max on the shoulder. "Yep. All yours, buddy."

Elijah squeezed between them and slid open the small window to let the stale air out and the fresh mountain breeze in. "There's a loft in the barn if you want to take it," he told Max.

The giant jock sneered down at Elijah. "Barn? For me and Gretchen? What are we, animals?"

"Have it your way," Elijah sighed, pulling back the top sheet. Two more mice raced off the bed and scrambled for safety.

"I'll take the barn," Max blurted. He dashed out of the room and clomped to the other bedroom.

Instantly Elijah found himself in a headlock, the familiar smell of George's discount deodorant crowding his sinuses as his bigger, badder buddy wrestled him onto the bed and nestled his knuckles against the top of his skull.

"Annie Rourke, hah? Why didn't you tell me?" he said,

burying Elijah in the pillows.

"Get off me." Elijah grunted and slipped out of George's grasp. He didn't want to talk about inviting Annie, not with George, not after that car ride, not *now*. "I gotta find some clean sheets."

He felt something crush beneath his sneakers. Looking down, Elijah found the floor was encrusted with pellets from dried mouse poo.

"And some traps."

CHAPTER THREE

Gretchen popped a wedge of neon green gum past her lips as she hoisted her last bag out of Felicity's trunk.

An upstairs window flew open. Max stuck out his head. "Gretchen, babe, get that fine ass up here. I just found out where we'll be spending the night."

"Okay," she shouted, surprised at the squeak of her voice. Max gave Gretchen a lurid wink before tucking his head back in the window.

She teetered under the weight of her many bags; three arrows slipped out from the quiver she shouldered. Gretchen groaned, dropped her bags and scrambled to re-pack her arrows.

"The hell are those?" Felicity asked, angling her tall, beautiful body beside the trunk and yanking out a bow. "And what's *this*?"

Gretchen giggled as she launched into her well-rehearsed resume. "Well, I won the state championship for the last three years running. I was just elected captain of the girl's varsity archery team and I thought I'd get in some target practice while I was—"

Felicity slid her backpack higher up her bony shoulder and yawned, "Whatevs." She stood back and began to look Gretchen up and down, which immediately put Gretchen on edge.

"You know," Felicity began, "Max is so happy to be with you. He is *so* in love with you. You're all he ever talks about."

"Oh, that's so sweet," Gretchen gushed.

Felicity wrapped her up in a tight hug. "We're going to be such good friends!"

Gretchen dropped her bags and felt the air slowly squeeze out of her lungs until all she could inhale was Felicity's perfume bomb. It smelled vaguely like a blown-out candle and used socks.

Felicity eased off the hug. "You know," she said, voice frowning, "I have a confession to make."

"You do? What?"

After a pregnant pause, Felicity confessed. "Max and I had a thing once. Are you okay with that?"

Gretchen smiled with relief. "Oh, that? He already told me all about it. Wasn't that, like, in the seventh grade?"

"Eighth," Felicity corrected, leaning in close as if sharing a secret. "And it was more than a thing. We were '*involved.*'" She supplied her own air quotes. "It was very intense, Gretchen. *Very* intense."

Max had told Gretchen all about her "fling" with Felicity, describing it as "six months of begging and six minutes of touching her boobs through her bra." Gretchen was pretty sure Felicity was the last thing on his mind this weekend, just as she was now sure Max was the *first* thing on Felicity's mind.

Gretchen cleared her throat. "But now you have George. You two are so cute together and he's so good for you—"

Felicity gave Gretchen's shoulders a squeeze.

It felt more like a pinch.

"It's nice to see Max with someone who appreciates him the way you do," Felicity interrupted, gritting her teeth together. "I'm afraid I was a bit too challenging and complex for him at the time."

Gretchen bit her tongue.

"He seems really happy with you… and that makes *me* happy." Felicity's voice had grown throaty and her eyes glazed over.

Gretchen involuntarily took a step back. "Yeah," she mumbled, picking her bags back up and hoping to make a speedy exit. "He's a really great guy."

"And so talented," Felicity agreed, inching closer. "He used to write me little notes in class. I saved every one." She looked around to see if anyone else could hear them before she turned her attention back to Gretchen. "He's so gifted, you know." She motioned with her hips.

Gretchen arched one eyebrow. "Oh?"

Felicity nodded enthusiastically. "And it certainly was a challenge…"

Gretchen raised the other eyebrow. "Uh-huh?"

Felicity shook her head and chortled under her breath. "Like anyone could get their hand around it…" Her voice drifted away, like the random look in her creepy, intense blue eyes.

Gretchen was thoroughly stumped. In fact, she was starting to become alarmed. She looked at Felicity directly and asked, "What are you talking about?"

Felicity stepped back, waving a hand before her. "Nothing, nothing. You should be fine… if, you know, you've been doing your exercises."

"*What* exercises?" Gretchen demanded, clearly exasperated.

Instead of answering her, Felicity had another question. "I don't mean to get personal but… you're a virgin?"

Gretchen nodded, regretting telling her that much.

"You're a *little* girl," Felicity said, overstating the obvious. Gretchen stood at five-foot two and weighed less than ninety pounds.

"Yeah? *And*?"

Felicity leaned over, a wicked smile splashed across her beautiful, crazy face, and whispered in her ear, "*I hope you stretched it out before coming here.*" She laughed as she trailed away, leaving Gretchen completely dumbfounded.

Stretch? Stretch *what*? What was she talking about? What could you possibly stretch…?

Oh. That. She hadn't thought about… *that*.

Gretchen didn't notice Max as he came bounding down the steps toward her.

"Hey," he huffed, breathless from running. "What's taking you so long? Need a hand with these?"

Gretchen, still punch-drunk after an intense ten minutes with Freaky Felicity, simply shook her head.

Max embraced her, standing a head taller, and nuzzled his face in her hair. "I can't wait for tonight. It's all I've been thinking about."

"Me too," she purred, sliding her eyes past his chest, down his waist and onto the front of his bulging jeans.

The bump was much larger than she remembered. In fact, it looked like the outline of a coiled snake hiding under a rug.

For the first time Gretchen wondered if she had her doctor's phone number handy.

CHAPTER FOUR

Elijah searched through Nana's wardrobe for a fresh comforter, one without moth holes or littered with rat droppings. He caught his reflection in the cracked mirror on the door. The part in his hair looked severe; Elijah tried to cover up his exposed scalp with a few stray hairs. He gave up after realizing it didn't make his face look any better.

He yanked a flannel comforter out from under a pile of hand-sewn blankets when he saw it—a double-barreled shotgun resting against a half-empty case of red shells. Probably used for hunting deer or duck, but for the life of him, Elijah couldn't imagine his Nana holding such a magnificent, violent beast, let alone firing it. It looked too large and lethal. He picked up one of the shells and inspected it; it was exactly the size and weight of something he imagined Elmer Fudd using in one of those Saturday morning cartoons he used to watch before the accident. Although the shells were old and dusty and a layer of grime came off on his fingers, they still felt dangerous.

A familiar voice bounced into the room. "Elijah?"

He jumped, slammed the wardrobe door shut and spun around, holding the comforter protectively as if he was naked underneath.

Annie stood in the doorway, luggage in hand.

"H-h-how long have you been standing there?"

"Long enough," she smirked and stepped into the room. She dropped a single black bag on the floor. "Is this my bed?"

"All yours." Elijah unfurled the comforter and tossed it onto the bed. "And so far as I know, one hundred percent rodent free."

"Glad to hear it." She sat upon the bed, palms down on the quilt, and crossed her endlessly long legs. "Comfy."

Elijah nodded proudly. "This was Nana's bed. I used to sleep in the hammock next door. My parents slept on the sofa downstairs, which is where I'll be sleeping."

Annie pouted her ruby-colored lips and patted the bed next to her, indicating he should sit down. Like a good boy, he lowered himself next to her, making sure there was a polite distance between them. He felt his armpits and palms fill with sweat. Still, he smelled her perfume—spicy, crisp, enticing. He felt her warmth too, although it may have been just his own personal heat waves bouncing off her and back onto him.

Annie studied the room. "Did you come here a lot when you were a kid?"

Elijah smiled, recalling the fonder memories of a time long gone. "Yeah. My parents would bring me here every summer. In fact, we were on their way here when they..."

Elijah's throat closed. It happened every time he brought up the memory.

Annie reached out and touched his arm. Her voice was kind as she said, "That must have been devastating for you, Elijah."

He nodded, avoiding her eyes. "Yeah. I thought the world had ended. It didn't, which was a great disappointment to me at the time..."

Elijah pondered telling her just how devastating it had been. The sleepless nights. The fevered dreams. The year he took off from junior high to home school because the sound of slamming lockers reminded him of the PVC pipes slamming through the windshield. Those deep long one-sided conversations with God, asking Him why and how could He have done such a horrific thing. He wanted to tell Annie all of it. She was right there, a few feet away, smiling back at him, not waiting to tease or threaten him or to punk or prank him. He wanted nothing more than to look into those deep green eyes and tell her everything he was feeling.

Instead he cleared his throat and said, "Nana wanted to

refurbish this place, but she never did."

Annie chuckled. "It's a good thing she didn't, Elijah. Your Grandma has shit for taste."

Before Elijah knew it he was laughing. Spontaneous, unforced laughter. He realized he did that a lot around her. Forgetting himself, he moved closer to her. "I remember my Dad would take me on these long hikes up the mountain. It would take all day and when we'd come down Mom would have this campfire going and together we'd all cool off in the lake."

"Oooh, great idea! Let's go for a swim. Before it gets dark."

Elijah's stomach flipped. "But, but I... I didn't bring my bathing suit."

George launched through the door and landed right in front of them.

"That's why God invented underwear!" he shouted.

Elijah rocketed three feet in the air and landed like a sack of potatoes; Annie vaulted into the air as a result. He stood abruptly, a blush rising to his face just as quickly. "H-h-how long have you been standing there?"

"Long enough to hear this girl make the best suggestion of the night."

Annie looked from George to Elijah. "I'm game," she added coyly, shoving Elijah's shoulder playfully, "if you are." She removed her sweater and shirt above her head and threw it onto the floor. A black lacey bra graced her chest. She threw Elijah a wink and scampered through the doorway and down the stairs, George following her, whooping and hollering all the way down the stairs and out the cabin.

Elijah sat on the bed and stared at nothing for the longest time, the room filled with silence, broken only by the gurgling sounds emitting from his stomach.

Elijah tiptoed down the front steps of the porch, feeling puny and pale with the towel tied under his rib cage. His white briefs clung tight to his body and no matter how hard he pulled, it would not go down past his groin area. He longed for one of those 1920s bathing suits his long-departed great-grandfather would have worn.

Outside, a strange humming noise that sounded like a wheezy air conditioner lingered in the air. But the cabin had no air conditioner. Heck, they were fortunate to have running water. No, this was a low, guttural humming. It sounded like someone imitating a cow...

Elijah turned and saw Felicity. She sat cross-legged, arms at her knees, meditating beside a tree trunk. Eyes closed, she stretched her head skyward with each "Om," or "*Awmn*," as she pronounced it. The length of her neck made her look like a giraffe reaching for leaves.

Then he heard a whizz of air followed closely by a sharp *twack*. Elijah followed the sound to the gravel driveway and watched in awe as tiny Gretchen stood, erect as an Olympian, dangerous as a hunter, bow in hand, the taut string drawn back. An arrow pierced a bull's eye set up near a cluster of pine trees. Rapidly, once, twice, three more times, she repeated the move; three more arrows joined the first in the target's center.

Dead center.

"Nice," Elijah found himself uttering.

Gretchen was startled to find an audience. She smiled and curtsied graciously before sliding another arrow into the bow and pulling back the string.

Max was hunched over a small fire, stick in hand, dangling a hot dog over the flames. He wore khaki baggies that looked like cargo pants and a gray tank top that clung to his sculptured chest like a second skin. He barely glanced at Elijah. Instead, he lifted the sizzling weenie from the flame and wagged it at Gretchen.

"Want one?" Max leered, offering her a salacious wink.

Gretchen gasped and released the arrow without her usual grace and poise. With a loud *thwunk*, the arrow impaled itself into the tree where Felicity was meditating, quivering a few feet above her head.

"The hell!" Felicity blurted, all evidence of *awmn* gone from her body. Max laughed as Gretchen rushed to apologize, which only made Felicity more red in the face.

Elijah used the pandemonium to race into the tree line that surrounded the lake.

George splashed near the floating deck in the middle of the lake. It had been tethered to the bottom for as long as Elijah could remember. He saw Elijah and waved him forward.

Tentatively, Elijah crept onto the dock.

"Where's Annie?" he called, as loud as he dared.

George shrugged. "I don't know, but the water's perfect. Come on in."

Elijah glanced around. To his left was a cluster of pine trees. To his right stood a small cluster of bushes, motionless. He let the towel spill around his ankles, nothing separating him from the cold alpine air but his undies, when a figure ran out of the bush, arms outstretched, and pushed him into the lake with an undignified *ker-plunk*.

Elijah splashed in the shallow water, desperate to cover what little of him remained above the water's surface, when he saw Annie standing above him, hands on her hips, a broad smile upon her lips. Her black bra and cut-off shorts were dripping wet.

"Nice tightie-whities," she said. "Race you to the raft."

Annie arched gracefully over his head and dove into the lake, barely making a splash. Without looking back, she swam toward the floating deck in the middle of the dark, cool water.

Elijah, never a strong swimmer on a good day and weaker still with one arm covering his privates at all times, flailed after her. When he caught up to Annie, she was gently circling the raft, doing the backstroke. Elijah clung to the deck's side, catching his breath. George helped him out of the water. Elijah, too exhausted to worry about his inadequate anatomy, collapsed on his back.

George raised himself up on one elbow and nudged him playfully. "So, how long have you been seeing someone behind my back?"

Elijah grinned in spite of his pounding chest. "I haven't been seeing her. I just met her this week."

"And what? You just asked her to come out here on a whim? Right out of the blue?"

"Yeah? So?" Elijah didn't want to tell George exactly how he had come to ask Annie out. There wasn't anything to tell. He was unlocking his crappy bike when he happened to see Annie walk by. Following her friendly hand wave to him, Elijah muttered only two words to her—"Would you?"—before she answered with "Yep," cutting him off. Was life really that easy?

Elijah sat up. He spied the pads of Annie's bra glide just above the surface of the water like twin shark fins.

George watched them too. He snickered.

"What?" Elijah asked.

"Nothing, man. She's great. I'm happy for you."

"Thanks," Elijah said uncertainly. There was something about the way George was watching Annie move—eyes glazed, jaw jutting forward—that made him uneasy.

Annie broke through the surface, treading water just out of earshot. Her hair was wet and slicked back, her pale skin almost ghostly above the black water.

George took his eyes off Annie's bobbing body for a rare moment and peered curiously at Elijah. "I just hope you know what you're doing, bro."

"Huh?"

"Yoo hoo," came Annie's voice from the lake, her hand dripping as she waved at them. "Elijah, the water's so warm. Come on in."

Elijah waved back but before he could beg off, she dove underwater, head first, her body arching through the water like a dolphin. For a moment, her backside hovered in the air.

George was immediately slack-jawed. "Holy shit! Will you look at that?"

Elijah gasped to see what George was referring to—a tattooed pentagram just above the crack of her butt. There was no mistaking it. It stood out against her milk white skin. In a flash it was gone, dashed beneath the surface as Annie came up for air, bubbly and bright.

George clapped Elijah on the back, beaming as if his friend had just scored the winning touchdown. "A tramp stamp. Dude, you are so *in*."

"W-what's that supposed to mean?"

George shook his head. "You haven't put the pieces together yet, have you?"

Elijah sat up, still dripping. "What pieces?"

"Let me see if I can paint you a picture, bro." He counted off his points on his fingers. "You don't know her. You just asked her out to a weekend in the mountains. With no TV. With you."

Elijah studied George's open palm, his four fingers extended. "Yeah? So? So what?"

George slapped him on the shoulder. "So what? So *congratulations*! You just invited the surest thing in Holy Ghost High!" He stood, his weight shifting the surface of the raft until Elijah was practically rolling over, and dove into the lake, splashing Annie and making her giggle.

Elijah contemplated ways of unhooking the raft to set sail for a distant land, a land where he wouldn't have to worry about girls with tramp stamps, when he felt a sudden chill in the air. He clasped both arms against his naked chest, shivering. A quick flash of lightning broke over the blue sky. From the water George and Annie pointed to something above him. Elijah looked up and squinted.

The object was small and dark and hurtling directly toward him at great speed. As it grew larger and larger, Elijah saw it was fat and green and had four legs and—

SPLAT!

Annie screamed, one hand over her mouth and one hand pointing at Elijah.

George looked disgusted. "Yo, dude, what's wrong

with your face?"

A frog, heavy and slimy, had collided and disintegrated atop Elijah's forehead. Amphibian blood and guts streamed down his cheeks. His eyes stung. His head rang and reverberated from the impact, like the inside of a bell.

A whistle sounded from above. Elijah looked up.

A second frog flattened itself across the bridge of his nose, knocking him off the raft and into the water.

George and Annie dove after him. The din of frogs plummeting through the air was constant now. Frogs splashed left and right as they hoisted Elijah above the water and dragged him to shore. Back on dry land, frogs littered the ground, guts and gore spitting out of their popped bellies, their tiny frog legs kicking the air.

Elijah glanced up and saw Max at a distance, oblivious to it all, staring into the fire.

George shouted at Max, "Dude, forget the hot dog. There are frogs falling from the—"

Just then, a flaming frog leapt from the fire and landed on top of Max's foot. Max shrieked like a third grader at recess, arms waving as he fell backwards. His head made contact with the edge of a tree stump, and he was out.

"Max!" George yelled. He tried to reach his jock pal, but a torrent of frogs fell, pelting him and Elijah as they shielded Annie from the deluge. The frogs burst on impact, covering Elijah's entire body with rancid, steaming guts. Annie wailed and covered her head.

The three found shelter under the nearest tree. Annie clung to Elijah's side, her body trembling as the wriggling and squirming frogs descended all around them. Elijah inhaled a deep breath and took in the devastation.

The blizzard of falling amphibians led to zero visibility. Their slick bodies dog-piled each other on the cabin's tin roof before sliding off and rolling onto a carpet of other frogs. Some frogs were cushioned by their broken brethren, others never made it past the high-velocity impact.

Felicity scrambled toward Max, her back taking a pounding. "Max!!!" she cried, doing the splits as both her legs flew out from under her, in opposite directions. "I'm coming, baby, hold on!!!!" The frogs rained so heavily they doused the fire.

Gretchen jumped from the cabin steps, towel in hand, and raced toward Max. She grabbed Max by one shoulder and placed the towel beneath his head just as Felicity joined her.

"The hell?" Felicity blurted to the pert young freshman.

But Gretchen was determined to save her boyfriend. She shouted at Felicity, "We've got to get him into the house. Now grab an arm or sit your ass down!"

They hoisted Max's massive, unconscious body up and away from the smoldering fire logs. A smear of blood from Max's head marked the stump. Elijah winced. The girls dragged Max to the cabin, frogs pelting them every inch of the way.

"Gross," Felicity screamed, kicking them away from Max's inert body and squashing them beneath her pristine white sneakers. "Get away, frogs! *Fuck off!*"

At last the girls got him under the shelter of the porch roof.

"Come on," Elijah shouted to Annie and George. "We have to make a run for it or we'll be no better off than Max."

George nodded and gunned it across the yard, not waiting to see if Annie or Elijah were behind him.

"Some friend," Annie grunted, grabbing Elijah's hand. They sprinted behind him.

The porch steps were slickened with frog guts and black blood. The cacophony of frogs pelting the tin roof overhead sounded like gunshots under water. Elijah and Annie held onto each other until they were inside. Max lay on the floor, bleeding from the head. Felicity and Gretchen were shouting at each other.

"Get some ice."

"Fuck you! *You* get some ice."

"Fine, give me the towel."

"Fuck you! *You* give me the towel."

Elijah, desperate for some illusion of control, could only shout back at them, increasing the noise volume among the chaos. "Guys, guys, can we please just GET IT TOGETH—"

Static pierced the air. Elijah rushed to cover his ears. George, Annie, Felicity and Gretchen each followed suit, cowering from the white noise.

The static ended and the radio sprang to life. An old-time religious sermon, canned and distant, boomed throughout the room:

> *"Then the Lord said to Moses, 'Tell Aaron, Stretch out your hand and your staff over the streams and canals and pools, and make frogs come up on the land of Egypt...'"*

The reverend's voice, worn and scratchy and hollow, had enough fire and brimstone left in it to shame anyone on the receiving end.

Elijah felt like he was eleven again.

> *"And Aaron stretched out his hand over the waters of Egypt..."*

The magic eye, pink and sharp, glowed intensely with the reverend's voice, as if the two were one and the same.

> *"... and the Lord did as Moses had asked. The frogs in the houses and courtyards and fields died off—"*

The radio shut itself off. The eye went dark. The roof

was silent but for the sound of the few remaining frogs sliding across it and onto the ground.

Max, with perfect timing, sat up, having missed the radio program and the frog rainfall. He saw Felicity and Gretchen standing above him, mid-stride, a bag of ice in Felicity's hand, a towel in Gretchen's, mouths agape and staring at the radio.

"Hey guys," he said, a chuckle in his voice, "what did I miss...?"

Max rubbed the back of his head and brought back a bloody hand.

He fainted.

CHAPTER FIVE

Elijah passed out the last of the quilted blankets from the cedar chest in front of the couch. He helped himself to the last grape soda from the cooler and sat down on a wicker chair by the fireplace. Felicity snuggled close to Max, the top of his head wound wrapped in bloody gauze, his face long and ashen. Across the coffee table, in a big puffy chair, Gretchen quietly fumed. George, clueless, and hoping to get even more so, lit a joint and passed it around. Annie declined. She sat on the rug next to the fireplace, her long legs crossed under the terry cloth robe she had grabbed from her room.

George exhaled a plume of acrid smoke and croaked, "Tell it to me again, Gretchen. Water sports?"

Gretchen rolled her eyes and leaned forward in her puffy chair, presumably to be closer to Max. "Not water sports. Water *spouts*. You know, like how a tornado on land scoops up everything that lies on its path? Well, a water spout is a tornado that forms above water. It can suck a whole lake dry and everything that lives in it. I saw it on the National Geographic Channel."

Annie shook her head gently, her profile soft and gentle in the crackling fire. "I don't know, Gretchen. Those were a *lot* of frogs."

Felicity nodded. "And it wasn't windy."

Max's eyes fluttered open beneath his tightly wound bandage. "It all seemed like some crazy Moses shit to me. Like one of the Seven Plagues of Egypt."

Elijah corrected him. "Ten. There are ten plagues."

Gretchen's eyes, already tea cup size, grew to saucers. "Ooh, you mean like flies, boils and locusts?"

"And the river of blood?" added Felicity.

Elijah put down his soda and sat up, suddenly eager to contribute. "The plagues were from God working through Moses to threaten the Pharaoh and his people. But there are a lot of references to frogs in the Bible besides in Exodus. And as for blood, there's mention of it in Genesis, Exodus, Psalms as well as in Revelations and Leviticus..." He trailed off, aware that everyone was staring at him with blank looks. He picked up a poker and stoked the fire, shrugging, "It's all there in the Bible."

Under his breath, he muttered, "If any of you actually bothered to read it."

Annie heard it. She laughed.

Elijah smiled back.

George relit his roach and blew out a generous cloud. "Well, I for one vote for water spouts."

Gretchen beamed, happy someone agreed with her.

Max nodded in agreement, "I do too. Makes the most sense, right?"

"Of course," George said in between puffs. "We'd be in real trouble if we started looking to the Bible for answers."

Elijah shot him a look. He was used to George's personal put downs, but this felt different. He let it go; the cabin was no place for a Bible discussion. The group had spoken: the radio was old and things fell from the sky every day.

Felicity waved a hand across the living room, wishing the whole drama away with a single gesture. "Whatever it was, what's important is everyone is safe."

She gave Max's thigh a tight squeeze.

Elijah wasn't the only one to notice.

Gretchen rose with finality, cleared her throat, looked pointedly at Max and said, "Hon, I think it's time we go."

Max, dazed as he was, got the message. He extricated himself from Felicity's hold, stood on wobbly feet and grumbled sheepishly, "Night, y'all."

Felicity stood abruptly and heaved Max to her bosom in a bear hug. "Night-night, Maxie. Don't do anything I wouldn't—"

The typically docile Gretchen yanked Max out of the cheerleader's clutches. Without a backward glance, the two left the cabin, the heavy front door slamming behind them.

George extinguished the last of his joint and stood. Holding out a hand to Felicity, he said, "I guess we'll head off too. Felicity, you want to... uh...?" He made an awkward gesture up the stairs.

Felicity sighed and glanced toward the door where Max had exited. "I suppose."

George stood at the foot of the stairs and eyed Felicity's shapely derriere as it slinked past him. He gave Elijah a wink and "Psst'd" him over.

Elijah got up shyly, leaving Annie to sip a beer alone by the fire. "What is it?" he whispered.

Glassy-eyed and fumbling with his hands, George reached into his pocket and pulled out a strip of condoms in a variety of colors. "Look, bro, I got a green one here. She'll dig it, trust me. Something about green just makes 'em go buck wild, you know—"

"Will you put that away!" Elijah hissed, shoving it back in George's pocket. "She's right there, four feet away."

Elijah turned around to find Annie had moved from her place by the fire to sit in the middle of the couch. Her robe was hiked up just a smidge, exposing the tops of her thighs.

George, with surprising dexterity, tucked the green condom in Elijah's shirt pocket. "Just be cool. Be yourself. And don't do anything *fat*."

———————

At first, Elijah paced; he pretended to search for something in his pants pocket, only to find a handful of lint. He gave up on the pocket search and made his way to the puffy chair away from the couch. Annie looked vaguely disappointed as he sat, but she hid it behind a swig from her bottle.

Elijah spied a jumble of bottles on top of the coffee table, needing something, anything, to drink.

"Wine cooler?" he offered, holding it out to her.

Annie half-smiled and shook her head. "Wine coolers make me throw up."

Elijah shrugged, twisted off the top and took a swig. It was sickeningly sweet and — ugh — warm. "I can see why."

Annie laughed, putting him at ease once again. Her hair was still vaguely damp from the shower she'd taken to remove the frog intestines. The collar of her robe was open just enough to reveal the start of her cleavage. The firelight illuminated her long, shapely form, casting shadows across her face and lifting little golden flecks from those amazing jade eyes. She rested the bottom of her beer bottle on her bare upper thigh.

He could stare at that thigh all evening.

When he looked up, he saw her staring at him, waiting for him to... do what? *What do I do?* He should say something. He needed to say something. *Yes, but what?*

Elijah scanned his thoughts and decided he would speak about the first thing that popped up in his head. He cleared his throat.

"You know... despite what everyone thinks, I'm not *that* religious."

Annie's eyebrows raised. "No?"

"No. I believe in abortion. I'm pro-marriage. And..." he trailed off, searching, reaching, "I recycle."

"Cool. Me too."

Elijah nodded, peeling away the label of his disgusting wine cooler and forcing another sip down. "It's just... I hate feeling like the leper of the group because I just happen to believe in something bigger than me, that's all."

Annie shrugged, and uncrossed then re-crossed her legs the other way.

Elijah almost fainted.

"Tell me about it," she snorted. "I wanted to be a nun."

Elijah choked on his drink. "What? Really?" She *had* to be pulling his leg.

Her nod was energetic, her eyes earnest. "What? You think you're the only believer in this cabin? Yep, I was going to be a bride of Jesus."

He wasn't sure if it was the half-a-wine cooler or the sudden admission that she'd wanted to be a nun, but Elijah got up and sat next to Annie on the couch. Annie seemed surprised, but pleasantly so.

"So what happened?" he asked.

"Scotty Johnson happened."

"Wait—what? You dated... *Scotty Johnson*?" Elijah knew Scotty Johnson as the oily-haired, acne-faced drop-out from school. He grew up with Scotty and could barely recall him speaking more than three words in a row, but he never saw Scotty without a girl, most likely because Scotty had a garage band.

Annie took a swig of beer and gazed back at him levelly. "We did more than just date."

"Oh," he nodded then realized, "Oh!"

Annie nodded. She seemed to have slid closer to him when he wasn't looking, close enough for Elijah to smell the rich, amber beer on her breath as she confessed, "Mistakes were made."

"But... why Scotty Johnson?"

"I was new in school. I was bored. I was impatient," she sighed, getting a faraway look in her eyes. She toyed lazily with one wisp of hair, wrapping it and rewrapping it around one finger. "I just couldn't stand being alone. I wanted something here and now and not have to wait for the infinite. I wanted to embrace life, not hide from it. I wanted to feel something real pressing against my skin instead of my life-size Raggedy Ann doll."

Elijah nodded, though he didn't quite get that last part.

Annie paused to steal courage from another sip of beer. "I thought it was love. It wasn't. I moved on."

"Wow... still... Scotty Johnson..."

"I said it was a mistake. You can drop it."

He smiled sheepishly. "Sorry."

"The point is," she continued, leaning over and talking softer, so no one else could hear, "I know what it means, being religious, but I hope you're not afraid of me or any feelings I might have for you. Or what we could do together. What I'm really saying is..."

She reached down, touched his knee… and squeezed.

Her touch froze him to the couch.

"If you like me, there's no reason to sleep alone."

The fire's shadows shimmered across her face, a face hovering inches from his. All he had to do was lean forward and their noses would be touching, their lips possibly kissing. But there was no way Elijah would make that happen. He wasn't going to make the first move. He didn't even know what the first move *was*. It crossed his mind that if he kept still long enough he would force her to kiss him first out of apathy. He hoped that plan would work. It was the only plan he had.

Annie did not kiss him. Instead, she rose and headed for the stairs. She paused at the banister to look back at him. He sat there, unable to move, unable to speak. She seemed both flattered by his reaction… and frustrated. Still, she smiled, gave a wink and strode purposefully up the stairs.

As soon as he heard the soft click of her bedroom door closing, Elijah bolted off the couch. He sprang for the front door, threw it open and stopped at the edge of the porch, desperately breathing in the rich, night air.

Frogs still littered the ground, their greasy, pebbly skin lit by the full moon. A scraggly moth flailed itself against the porch light directly above Elijah.

Tink, tink.

A breeze chilled the air, but Elijah didn't feel it. His face was flushed and his skin was warm. In fact, his whole body glowed as all the pressures from the weekend seemed to lift off his shoulders. He felt… confident.

No, that wasn't it.

He felt… relieved.

No, that wasn't it either. What was it?

He felt… wanted. Yes, that was it.

And Lord, he was ready.

CHAPTER SIX

The temperature inside the barn was almost as frosty as the outside air. The loft space at the far end, past the empty rows of horse stables and hay bales, was no less chilly. And yet, Max had never felt warmer when Gretchen unbuttoned her shirt. She stood next to the mattress, in profile, nervous about being naked for the first time with a man. She wore size extra-small panties and white knee socks, one leg crossed in front of the other, her toes playing footsies with each other. Moonlight streamed through the crude planks behind her and blended with the steady flame of the old-fashioned oil lantern Max had hung from an available nail. The combined glow turned her young petite body to sweet cream, her innocent eyes looking up at him every few minutes with an *is-this-okay?* glance.

"Come here," he croaked, his throat tight with desire.

Her skin was cold in the barn's drafty chill as she fell into him, seeking his warmth as he sought hers. Max grew hard as they wriggled atop the mattress. He rolled beside her, not wanting to hurt her, and she giggled.

"Something funny?" he asked.

"No, nothing, it's just..." Her voice was soft and high-pitched with excitement and anticipation. "I can feel it against me. Do you think, before we, you know... could I see it?"

Max smirked and tried to laugh it off. "You're kidding me, right?"

Gretchen propped herself on one elbow, breasts so small and firm they barely moved. "Actually, I'm not."

"What, you mean, I should just... whip it out, like some science experiment?"

She nodded, eyes dark, no trace of a smile. "I want to know what I'm in for."

He felt it shrink with every word. "Is this a deal breaker?"

Gretchen sat up, cross-legged, her hands folded before her as if she was waiting for the reptile show at the zoo to begin.

"This is all so formal," Max sighed and, before he could lose any more girth, yanked off his boxer shorts and let it fly.

He saw her cock her head to the side, like a dog who had heard a high-pitched noise, until a wide grin stretched her mouth.

"Well... that's a relief."

"*Relief?*"

She shrugged those delicate, bare shoulders. "Yeah, I mean, the way Felicity described it, I'd need forceps and a forklift to fit it in, but I've seen bigger on the internet."

Gretchen lay on her back, stripping her tiny pink panties off with little emotion. "Come on. Let's do it."

Max shook his head, unrolling his condom before sliding above her. "Well, if you insist…"

A moan escaped her lips as he entered her. She kissed him, greedily, fingers clutching his shoulders. Her legs wrapped around his waist, inviting him in almost desperately.

"Dang, girl, let's take it easy…"

Gretchen grunted and spun him over on his back without missing a beat… or an inch. "Listen stud, if I'm giving you my v-card, you're *taking* my v-card. This is *my* night!"

———————

Felicity finished brushing her teeth in front of the water-stained bathroom mirror. Her hair was back and up, the way she knew George liked it. She wore the flimsy pink tank top that started off at the top of her boob job she had at sixteen and stopped just above the six pack abs she worked so hard to get. After wiping her mouth she pulled a prescription bottle from her cosmetic case, which contained her last two pills. She took them out and carefully placed them on the edge of the sink, as was her custom. There was a crusty cup in a holder. No way was she going to drink out of *that*. The plan was to pop the pills in her mouth, scoop up a drink of water and swallow them down, airplane bathroom style. But first, she wanted to enjoy the edginess that accompanied her last few minutes before narcotizing herself into sleep. Her mind was faintly buzzing with paranoid thoughts and random musings, and she knew within ten minutes of taking them, the pills would dull her into the nice, placid plaything George preferred.

That the world prefers, an inner voice said. *But that's not the real you, is it?*

Felicity smiled wickedly to herself, giving in to the thoughts: *The real you is a duchess. You were born to be a duchess and one day you shall be one, in some far away land that no one could ever point out on a map, and you shall have babies that grow up to be kings and queens, and the country's dollar bill will have a picture of your face and under your chin, displayed on a wavy-like scroll, it will read "the Beloved Mother of Our Country."*

Not bad for a cheerleader, she nodded to herself.

Felicity leaned on the windowsill and gazed out at the barn where Max and Gretchen had disappeared to earlier. The barn was large and sagging, with two windows facing the cabin. She gasped when she saw the pair, silhouetted by the lamp light, clutched in an amorous embrace.

Felicity stared—and stared and stared, torn between desire and jealousy, passion and anger, until her heavy breathing fogged up the glass in front of her. When she finally tore herself away, her hip brushed against the edge of the sink...

... and she saw her last two pills tumble down the drainpipe. Panic-stricken, she reached after them, digging her fingers down the drain, but the pills were lost down the old cabin pipes.

Felicity thought of the long weekend ahead, the edge that would overtake her, the voices that would haunt her, the danger she would face...

And she smiled.

"Babe?" George called from the other room. "You about ready? 'Cause I sure am... and I don't know how long I can stay ready."

Felicity's smile morphed into a frown and, as sweetly as sugar, called out, "Just a minute." She pinched her cheeks, lifted her breasts, and pranced into the room on bare feet.

George lay in the hammock, shirt off, jockey shorts still on, swinging like an ape in a zoo.

"I can't believe we got the hammock," she exclaimed, stomping toward him.

"It was the only rat-free room in the place."

"And, what, that little Jesus-freak-you-call-a-friend gets to be busy in a nice, cozy bed?"

Felicity seethed, pacing the length of the hammock,

until George reached out to take her hand.

"Relax, babe." His voice was confident and cocky, just the way she liked it. "Think of it this way. You haven't made it until you've made it in a hammock."

George's face was hopeful, and handsome too. She had to admit that. While he was no Adonis like Max, he was tall and firm and fit and, if he would just shut up, she could imagine herself with her old flame.

Yes, said the voices in unison. *Yes, that's the ticket!*

Felicity undressed; she liked the way he looked at her naked body, staring in silence, as if he could pull her close to him just by using his thoughts.

If he had any, a voice cracked.

She shushed the voice in her head.

"What was that, babe?" George asked.

"Nothing, dear," Felicity blurted, realizing her shush had slipped beyond the confines of her head and landed in the bedroom.

George pulled her close and planted a kiss, thick and heavy, on her lips. He was warm, regardless of the chill in the drafty room. She slid in beside him and soon they were swinging in the hammock together. After some clumsy fumbling he got on top of her, lifted her legs and pounded away at her, as romantic as a dog in heat, and just as gentle. The hammock creaked as it swayed back and forth, back and forth. It was made of old rope which scratched her naked backside.

"Oooh, baby, what'd I tell you?" George grunted, eyes closed, smiling, pumping away.

The combination of the motion and his sweet talk became more than she could take. "Would you hurry up and finish? I'm getting seasick in this thing!"

No sooner did she say the words than he gasped, shivered and collapsed onto her. One hundred and fifty pounds of sweaty moron.

"When I said hurry up, I didn't mean *'forget to pleasure me.'*"

"It was too tight, anyway."

Felicity slugged him, hard, on his visible rib cage.

"The condom, I mean!" he squeaked out, gasping for air.

She shoved him to the side and reached for her robe. Somewhere in the barn Max was plying his wares with the freshman virgin while Felicity's night, her big weekend, was already over. The darkness overtook her, swifter than ever. Already George had his hands behind his head, drifting to sleep.

Felicity mourned her two last pills and began to weep, silently, next to him. The shuddering through her body sent ripples through the creaking hammock as the young couple gently rocked into sleep.

Elijah reached the top of the stairs. Cautiously, he raised

his hand to knock on the door. On cue, it creaked open, haunted house-style. Rather than a ghost or demon waiting to attack him, there was only Annie, looking demure but inviting on the other side of the door. She was in panties, no bra, and a white button-down shirt, half-open. Her hair was swept back, her legs and feet bare as she shut the door behind him. He had no choice but to follow as she drew him near, hands warm. Their lips met and they kissed, briefly, passionately. He felt the familiar stir down below when she pushed him away, teasingly. She threw herself onto her back upon the bed, her shirt popping open, exposing her bare chest and black panties.

Elijah's eyes nearly popped out of his skull.

Annie pulled him onto her warm, willing flesh. She plunged her tongue into his mouth. He had heard of French kissing before, but now in practice he wondered how to kiss back. He barely knew what to do with *one* tongue in his mouth, let alone two.

And then there was her scent. Her scent was intoxicating, yet vaguely... familiar.

"What's that smell?"

Her voice was soft as she replied, "I helped myself to your grandmother's perfume."

The perfume bottle sat on the nightstand next to the bed. The jar was old, like everything else in the cabin, made of frosted glass with purple and blue tints, bulging in the middle like a genie's bottle, the diamond shaped stopper lying nearby. A scented candle, infused with red and pink, glimmered beside it.

He turned back to Annie. She had let her hair down.

"I leave nothing to chance, pretty boy."

Elijah smiled, but before he could say or do anything else, she pulled him close once more and ran her fingers through his hair. His eyes darted from the hollow of her throat to the swell of each breast to her small, taut tummy. With no warning, she yanked off his shirt off and bit his left nipple.

"Ow!" he howled, surprised by the pain.

"Pain and pleasure go hand in hand," she said, eyes dilated.

He found this version of her intoxicating and wild, and most surprising, he was eager to submit to her demands.

In one deft move Annie yanked the belt from his jeans and tossed it at his bare chest. "Tie me up," she demanded, offering the sash from her robe for her second hand.

Elijah's voice was shaky, anxiety mixed with anticipation. "What? Really?"

He did as he was told. Annie lay there, half-naked, writhing on the double bed, skin glistening with sweat when something flashed in his peripheral vision.

A large man stood in the corner. Watching them.

Elijah shook his head, blinked. Maybe there was something in his eye. He looked again.

The man was still there, hands clasped in front of him.

He was dressed in all black, save for a white collar. His face was worn and leathery, and his eyes…

Elijah wasn't sure he *had* eyes.

A vice-like grip seized his rib cage. Annie squeezed him with her legs, her arms outstretched and fastened to the bedpost. She settled low on the mattress for leverage and urged him close with an unabashed hike of her knees.

"Take off your pants," she commanded.

Elijah turned back to the corner. The mysterious man was gone, replaced by Nana's standup coat rack where Annie's black jacket hung like a shadowy torso.

His hands trembled as he yanked off his jeans.

"Your underwear, too," she said, panting.

He immediately flashed back to his first time showering after gym class. "You first," he insisted.

"How am I supposed to do that?" she chuckled throatily, wriggling her bound hands for emphasis.

His hands shook as he reached for the lacy waistband of her panties. Annie quivered beneath his touch. Before he could slide the fabric down her thighs, she clamped his hips between those surprisingly strong thighs of hers and yanked him toward her. Her eyes were closed as she licked her lips and screamed, "Take me, Elijah! I can't wait any longer!"

She was grinding against him now, the bed moving frantically, the headboard hitting the wall like a bass drum in a fast march. Their movement shifted the nightstand

and upended the open perfume bottle. The contents spilled all over the table and onto the floor.

Nana's scent hit Elijah in a bizarre wave of nostalgia and disgust.

The candle wobbled in its holder, rocking to and fro from Annie's rodeo-like bucks. He reached for the waxy base, but it fell before he could reach it. He heard the *whoosh* of the perfume puddle beside the bed as it burst into flame.

Adrenaline dumped into his veins.

Annie gasped and slid out from under him. "Oh my God! UNTIE ME! UNTIE ME!"

Her desperate wails hit him square in the gut. He wanted to wretch.

Heat rose. The fire scorched the dry-tinder floors and raced up the window curtains. It incinerated the rocking chair and lit up the clothes they had left in a pile.

Elijah struggled to loosen the belt loop, but the heat made the leather belt sticky, the buckle nearly untouchable. His fingers scrambled through the burn. The fastener wouldn't budge.

"Help me!' Annie squealed.

"I can't." Elijah scanned the room for anything that would help.

There was only the man in black. The stranger was back, hands clasped, his gaze riveted on Elijah.

Annie wrestled until the entire bed post splintered free.

A jagged chunk of wood slammed into Elijah's eye. He screamed as the post sank through his socket like a warm knife into butter. The pain detonated inside his skull and his vision went black and he tumbled in free fall—

Right off the front porch.

He hit the ground hard, his hands beating invisible flames from around his body, but there was nothing there.

He reached for his forehead to yank out the bedpost.

Nothing there.

Elijah sat up. The forest was dark. The lake lapped gently against the shore. Hundreds of dead frogs lay all around him, and, he felt, underneath him.

It had been a dream, of course. A second nightmarish vision in less than twenty-four hours.

A second message from God?

The *tink, tink, tink* continued from the porch, only much louder and more insistent. Elijah looked up to find nearly a dozen moths circling the porch light, dashing in and out. One flew too close to the lamp and singed its fragile wings. Useless, it dove to the floor, dying in a smolder of flames.

Elijah watched the smoke curl from its blackened body.

Tink, tink, tink.

The radio in the living room crackled to life. An old, familiar church hymn oozed out:

> *"Are you washed in the blood,*
> *In the soul-cleansing blood of the Lamb?*

Are your garments spotless?
Are they white as snow?
Are you washed in the blood of the Lamb?"

He knew the song. Every word, every note of that song was etched into his brain. It was the same song that rose from the mangled car speakers and serenaded his parents' death all those years ago.

Elijah stumbled his way to the porch and stared past the open door. Inside, the magic eye simmered — glowing bold then diminishing before glowing bold again — in rhythm to the tune.

If an eye could dance, Elijah thought, *this is what it would look like.*

The hymn ended in a burst of static. An announcer's scratchy voice took over. "The Radio Church of God continues with the Reverend Bob Anderson." The voice of Reverend Bob cut in, stern and preachy, stiff as nails and just as unyielding:

> *"As the gnats infested man and beast, the magicians said to Pharaoh, 'This is the finger of God.'" Yet Pharaoh remained obstinate and would not listen to them, just as the Lord had foretold..."*

Elijah entered the room and, trance-like, walked toward the radio.

He didn't remember making the decision to move.

The station signal weakened in a hiss of static as he approached, then charged alive as Reverend Bob's voice blared:

> *"Early tomorrow morning present yourself to Pharaoh when he goes forth to the water, and say to him: Thus says the Lord: 'Let my people go to worship me. If you will not let my people go, I warn you, I will loose swarms of—'"*

Elijah snapped off the radio. The glow inside the magic eye receded until it was a distant speck.

From the top of the stairs, behind a half-open bedroom door, Annie's tender voice called out, "Elijah, are you coming up?"

It was at that moment when they heard Max's screams coming from the barn.

CHAPTER SEVEN

Gretchen's nostrils flared with each snore, her open mouth emitting guttural sounds that reminded Max of what she sounded like when at last she came. And that was just the first time. The minute he was ready to go again, she had assaulted him, demanding more, faster, harder, again.

Max gently removed Gretchen's snoring head from his sore, sweaty arm. He winced just moving. He slunk to the side of the barn, as far from her as he could get without standing. His belly was sore from her riding him like a bucking bronco, his back was sticky with blood from where she had raked her nails when, at last, she allowed him on top.

No way the chick was a virgin. No way.

Shrunken and naked, scratches on his shoulders and chest and thighs, he reached for his shorts. It was buried under Gretchen's backside. He'd be damned if he was going to wake her up before it was absolutely necessary.

Max sat with his back against the barn wall and watched Gretchen, her arm draped across her chest, her concave stomach rising gently with each breath, when a faint buzzing noise circled close to his ear. He waved a hand and noticed a fly drifting in and out between him and the sleeping Gretchen.

The insect settled on Gretchen's chin.

Max looked on with lazy fascination as Gretchen exhaled a mighty snore, inhaled a huge gust of air and, with it, the fly.

Gretchen sat up immediately, choking, clutching her throat. Blinking, her eyes focused on Max. Her expression was wild, dazed.

Max reached for her bare shoulder to comfort her. "Honey, it's okay. You just swallowed a fly."

Gretchen sputtered and coughed, hacking and wheezing.

Max's nerves spiked. He crept forward to help her. "Gretchen? Honey? You okay?"

Her skin went from pink to red to blue, her eyes bulging, panicking, fearful. She wasn't breathing, couldn't breathe, her fingers pale at her throat.

"Gretchen? *Gretchen!*"

He moved behind her, still naked. He slapped her back, harder and harder as she gasped, frantically, for air. Max slammed his hand, open palmed, between Gretchen's shoulder blades. With a spurt, the fly popped out, landing on the floor in a heaping glob of phlegm. Gretchen sucked in huge gulps of air.

Max sat back, relieved, watching her shoulders heave as she caught her breath. "Feeling better?" he asked, wiping a bead of sweat from his eyes.

Gretchen nodded, eyes grateful, but something was wrong. Her delicate little neck pulsed and swelled and engorged to a startling girth as if it had been jacked with a basketball pump. Her mouth constricted to a tight circle and she vomited out a projectile stream of... buzzing, living flies. The swarm streamed into the air.

Max screamed as a second wave filled her throat and, again, she spewed flies. They took flight in a black cloud, hundreds, thousands thick, as the sound of buzzing filled the barn.

A trail of rotting black fluid dripped from Gretchen's mouth onto the hay-covered floor. The fluid was teeming with maggots.

A third wave burst forth. This time, she hit the bulls-eye of Max's face.

Max wiped the flies and gunk from his face and bolted. Gravity seized his body. His stomach flew into his throat as he stumbled off the loft, falling two stories onto a haystack. The landing emptied his lungs of air. He rolled over, gasping, and saw a pitchfork sticking out of the hay bale, mere inches away.

Had he been wearing underwear, he might have

checked it.

Max rolled onto his back. A blur filled his vision. Gretchen landed on him, her face on top of his, her eyes black as pitch. She opened her gaping maw and spewed forth another violent wave of swarming black flies. They stung Max's face like a living sandstorm.

His feet connected with her stomach. A loud *oomph* escaped her body. He tumbled off the haystack and hit the barn floor running. At the barn doors, he paused only long enough to crack them open and slide through.

The cold night air blasted his naked torso. Through the crack in the door he spotted Gretchen scuttling across the barn floor on all fours like a crab.

Max slammed the barn doors shut and pinned his back against it. She pounded on it relentlessly. His bare feet sank deep into the packed dirt outside the barn door. He felt himself giving way until he heard his name and found Elijah, Annie, George and Felicity barreling toward him.

Felicity reached him first. "What did that bitch do to you?"

Her eyes trailed south. Max remembered he wasn't wearing anything. He cupped his manhood.

"Max, what's going on?" George shouted.

Out of breath, he cowered, naked as a baby, as the pounding grew louder, more insistent.

"What's in there? A bear?" Elijah asked, shoulder pressed to the door.

Max shook his head and huffed, "Gretchen... flies... scary *Exorcist* shit..."

Elijah and George shared a look of disbelief when the incessant pounding on the doors stopped.

The group stood silent, cautious, waiting for the worst. Elijah reached for the door.

"No!" Max shouted, retreating, his hands on his groin, Felicity following behind.

Annie joined Elijah and they swung the barn doors wide.

The barn was dark now, utterly devoid of light. Even the moonlight seemed unable to penetrate the broken and grimy windows on either side of the loft. Hay snapped beneath footsteps from some invisible corner as Gretchen emerged into the light.

Her black hair was mussed with sweat. Her face was clean, with nary a trace of maggots or black puke juice on her lips. She twirled a single strand of hair, Max's tank top flowing to her knees, and was surprised to see them all assembled there.

"Hey guys. Why so weird? I swallowed a fly."

CHAPTER EIGHT

"I saw her! She was a demon!"

Max, clothed in one of George's throwaway shirts and a pair of work jeans, paced in front of the couch where George and Felicity sat, a seat cushion between them.

Gretchen, draped in one of Nana's quilts, flashed him a murderous look. "I am *not* a demon! You take that back."

Max threw up his hands. "No? Then what was all that projectile fly vomiting and all those maggots and shit exploding from your mouth? You gonna tell me it was something you ate?"

Gretchen made an *eeewww* face. "Don't be ridiculous. You know I don't eat solids."

Max's nostrils flared. "You had two black eyes and you vomited evil all over me."

Annie poked absently at the dying embers of the fire. "Maybe a nest of mosquitoes got disturbed while you two were doing it."

"That got in her *mouth*?" Max snapped. "I know what I saw… this girl is possessed by the devil!"

Gretchen's eyes narrowed. "Wait a minute. Are you pissed because I was on top first? That's what this is about, isn't it?"

Elijah and Annie shared an exhausted look. Their eyes telegraphed, *Is this really happening*?

Max aimed a finger at Gretchen from across the room. "No girl moves like you move their first time. V-card, my ass."

"Why you—"

"Hey, hey now," George interrupted, waving his hands. "Relax, you guys. You're among friends."

Max's eyes grew wide again. "Friend? Friend? I *was* your friend until you took me and my girl to a haunted house in the mountains."

"This place is not haunted," George said, trying to placate his friend. "Tell him, Elijah."

Elijah barely heard. He was staring at the radio. It was glowing prettily from the dark side of the room, providing a gentle backdrop of 1920s dance music to the crude arguing.

"Elijah?" George asked, more forcefully this time.

Elijah snapped out of it and glanced at his friend. "Huzzawhatcha?"

George shook his head in disgust. Annie came to Elijah's side. "What's wrong, Elijah?"

"Nothing. It's just..."

"What, buddy?" George asked between concerned glances at Felicity and Max.

"The radio."

Felicity rolled her eyes. "I know. That station sucks."

Elijah ignored her. "No, I turned it off before I went outside... it just... it just turned on again, by itself, while we were arguing..."

One by one, each looked toward the radio. The magic eye glared back at them, ever-present, watchful.

"So turn it off, Elijah." George commanded, not moving.

Extending a trembling hand, Elijah inched toward the radio. As his fingers reached the knob, the music cut out and a deafening wave of static shot through the room like a sonic boom.

Elijah fell to his knees, holding his ears. Others screamed or jumped for cover.

Mid-squelch, the static stopped. The radio's magic eye burned laser-bright as the voice of Reverend Bob filled the room:

> "Then the Lord said to Moses and Aaron, 'Take a double handful of soot from a furnace, and in the presence of Pharaoh let Moses scatter it toward the sky. It will then turn into fine dust over the whole land of Egypt...'"

"Shut it off!" shouted Felicity, her hands clasped over her ears.

Elijah reached for the knob and snapped it off.

The reverend's voice continued to bellow through the room, uninterrupted:

> "'... and cause festering boils on man and beast throughout the land.'"

"TURN IT OFF!" Felicity shrieked.

"I'm trying!" Elijah twisted the knob over and again, repeatedly. Reverend Bob preached through each time:

> "So they took soot from a furnace and stood in the presence of Pharaoh. Moses scattered it toward the sky, and it caused—"

Before Felicity could scream at him a third time, Elijah spotted the electric cord sprouting from the back of the radio. With one pull, he yanked it from the socket.

The radio went dark. The magic eye closed and the room filled with silence once again.

Max curled on the couch, legs pulled to a fetal position. "I was right. This is some angry God shit right here."

"Will you zip it, Max?" blurted George, all patience gone. "It's an old radio for Christ's sake. Get a hold of yourself."

This time Elijah was on Max's side. "It's not the radio."

Annie put the fireplace poker down. "What is it then?"

Elijah peered slowly out the window. There, hanging low over the lake, was the moon. It was completely full, bright as a spotlight and achingly sinister. From an early age, Nana had taught Elijah to be extra good around a full moon. *"God uses the moon as a keyhole from which to spy on His children."*

George had heard Nana say it several times. When he saw what Elijah was looking at, he crowed. Loudly. "Oh come on, Elijah! This is a bit much, even coming from you."

"Think about it, George. Just think for a minute."

George placed his hands on his hips. "God? You think *God* is fucking with us? Why? For what?"

"For *THIS!*" Elijah yelled, waving his hands around the room. "For all of this—the drinking, the pot, the whatever-is-happening-upstairs-and-in-the-barn. For lying to our parents. *Everything*. We shouldn't be here. None of us should be here."

He faced the group. None could look him in the eye.

"George, you knew I never wanted to come until you forced me and now that everything's gone to crap, I think we should cut our losses and go."

Max and Gretchen grumbled. Felicity nodded. Even Annie seemed resigned to packing up and cutting loose.

George was incredulous. "Go? I don't know about you

all, but I'm having a terrific time." As if to prove it, he snuggled up to Felicity and wrapped his arm around her shoulder. Her look of disapproval didn't stop her from letting it stay there. "Look, you want a reason? Here it is— we're high up in the mountains. Frogs and flies are *natural* phenomena. God's not doing this to us, it's nature."

"Well, right now, it seems nature is kicking our asses," Elijah said, somewhat dejected.

"Look, Elijah," said George. "We're stoned, we're tired, and more than a little fucked up. I say we all get a little rest."

Gretchen nodded. "I agree with George. Besides, why would God punish us for something as silly as *sex*?"

Felicity glanced at Gretchen—and screamed.

Annie screamed next, covering her mouth.

George scrambled backward. Max jumped in the air.

Elijah, late on the draw, was the last to see what had happened to the poor freshman's face—Gretchen's flesh was covered with red, pink and throbbing, pus-filled, festering boils.

Max, not waiting for a second look, grabbed the first set of keys he found on the kitchen table and bolted through the front door.

"Hey!" Felicity shouted, spotting the dangling "F" hanging from the chain in his hand. "Hey, asshole! Those are my keys!"

The gang chased after Max, leaving Gretchen to use the last of strength to stumble to her feet. Her head felt like twenty pounds of crap shoved into a five pound bag and her face stung, hot and itchy, like the world's worst sunburn.

But aside from that, she felt fine.

Gretchen tripped her way through the screen door and onto the porch in time to hear Felicity's car engine rev up. Her friends surrounded the Beamer, pounding on its boxy windows and begging for Max to stop. No one shouted louder than Felicity, who seemed to care more about her ride than being abandoned.

"That's my car!" she screamed, beating on the driver's side door.

George clung to the hood. "Don't do it, dude. You can't leave us here!"

Gretchen pressed her face against the passenger side window. Grease from her ruptured pores smeared the glass. Her breath fogged the glass. Tears struggled to squeeze through her engorged eyelids.

"Max!" she cried, "You can't leave without me!"

Inside the car, Max screamed. He floored the accelerator, nearly running over George. Engine roaring, the car sped forward, spitting gravel, dirt and bark.

"Max!" Gretchen screamed, holding her chest, sobbing.

George reached down for a rock and heaved it at the

back window. The window splintered into a giant spider web before shattering.

Felicity had someone new to scream at.

George sprinted toward the blinking brake lights when the car's radio dial lit up with a hundred-decibel note of static that overpowered the engine and the raining gravel and the yelling. It was the same station that kept turning on and off in the cabin, the same Reverend Bob with the booming voice and religious warnings. The voice thundered down the road with the retreating car as the rest struggled to keep up:

> *"... Moses scattered it toward the sky, and it caused festering boils on man and beast..."*

The car slowed. George caught up first. He was about to grasp the door handle when Max turned on the headlamps.

Everyone, Max included, saw the tree at the last minute, too late to swerve away.

The front of the car crumpled itself around the base of the tree. Glass shattered. Metal screeched. Steam sizzled from beneath the hood. A great, white explosion of dust and nylon filled the driver's side.

George pulled open the door.

Max lay face-down in the air bag, unconscious.

The radio light fought for life for a few lingering

seconds before it vanished into darkness.

CHAPTER NINE

"I... I want to see," Gretchen babbled.

Annie ran a washcloth under the water in the bathroom sink. "No, Gretch, you don't—"

Gretchen pushed Annie out of the way to look into the mirror—and immediately wished she hadn't. Her head had puffed up to the size of a fish bowl, her skin an endless series of bumps and sores and welts and warts and boils.

"It's... it's my fault," she sobbed, avoiding Annie's eyes. "I never knew I was allergic to bug bites."

"Gretchen, no one is *this* allergic." Annie pressed the washcloth gently across her cheek when Gretchen turned back to the mirror, suddenly inspired.

"Maybe, if I pop a few of these blisters, the swelling will go down!"

Annie yanked Gretchen's arm and led her down the hall. "No."

"Let me just pop one," she gushed breathlessly.

"No."

"But they *sting*."

They stopped at the top of the stairs and stared at the scene below them. Max was on the couch, an ice pack on his nose, his head resting on Felicity's lap. Gretchen did a double take to be sure. He was looking up at Felicity, a childlike tone to his voice.

"I freaked, okay?" he said. "I just didn't feel like being here when the next plague hit."

The cheerleader ran her fake nails through Max's curls and cooed, "There, there, it's okay, Maxie."

George paced in front of the pair, barely concealing his disgust. "Classic. If I was the one who busted up your car you'd have had my head."

Felicity cut her eyes at him. "Max thought his girlfriend was a demon. It's different."

Gretchen bit her lip to stop from screaming. In doing so, she burst one of her boils and her mouth filled with a sour, salty fluid. She spit it out onto the floor.

Annie started to descend the stairs, but hesitated a few steps down when she realized Gretchen wasn't following. "Aren't you coming?"

Gretchen shook her head and lowered herself to the top step. She already felt like the pariah of the party. They didn't need a reminder that her face started it all.

Annie made a straight line to the fireplace where Elijah

stood. She warmed her hands by the fire and asked, "Elijah, what's the next plague?"

Elijah scratched behind his ear and stared at the darkened radio. "Well, they're not exactly happening in Bible order..."

George stopped pacing long enough to ask, "Come on, Annie. Don't tell me you believe in that nonsense."

"It's *not* nonsense, George," said Elijah, his tone defensive. "It happened. Once. In the Bible. If you read it once in awhile, you'd know that."

George waved a hand, scoffing. "And if you wash your hair on a Tuesday it won't rain on Friday. I don't believe in that crap, Elijah."

Elijah stepped forward, suddenly red in the face. "*What* crap, George?"

Gretchen felt the tension in the room, already thick, press against her chest.

George looked his friend in the eye. "I don't believe in any of it."

The little dude flinched. "W-w-w-w-w-what do you mean?"

"I don't believe there is a God. Period. All right?"

"Come on George, you know that's not true. I've been sitting beside you in mass every Sunday since I've known you."

George rolled his eyes. "I only go to mass so my Mom will buy me a car. That's the deal we have."

Elijah's lip trembled. "Wait... you mean... you don't believe... *at all*? Not even a little bit?"

Elijah searched the faces around the room.

"Does no one else here believe?"

Gretchen, never one to actually *read* the Bible, answered him as honestly as she could. "My parents pushed me into it."

Felicity shrugged. "The school is near my house."

Max sat up, clutching his head, and said, "I don't know what I believe anymore." He looked over at Gretchen on the stairs and added, "After what I saw happen to that thing over here, I'm open to anything."

"*Thing?*" Gretchen wailed in a weak voice, her heart breaking. Again.

George, unaffected, launched into Elijah. "Look... *you're* the one who needs to believe in God. You need to believe because it gives you comfort. Ever since your parents died you needed to know that someone was responsible for that, that someone was in charge... Well, I'm sorry to break it to you, but there's no one out there. There's *nobody watching us*. And I'm sorry you're an orphan, but God didn't do it. Shit just happens. And right now, this evening, we're covered in it. So do us all a favor, willya? Knock it off with all the God shit."

The room fell silent.

Elijah gulped.

They could all hear it.

White as a sheet, he turned to Annie. "You, too?"

Annie looked from Elijah to Gretchen then back to Elijah. Her voice was firm. "You know what I believe? I believe Gretchen needs medication. Is there a pharmacy nearby?"

His shoulders slumped as he gave up. "The nearest would be the rest stop back on the interstate."

Annie's eyes bulged. "That's like thirty miles from here."

"We're in the mountains, remember? There's nothing else around." Elijah looked toward Gretchen. "Can it wait 'til morning?"

Gretchen wanted to say, *It feels like a hundred ants are digging into my flesh, but I'm sure I can spend the night not wanting to tear my face off.* Instead, she gulped and shook her plus-sized head.

"My car is around back. I'll go." Annie started for the door.

Elijah blocked her. "No. I'll go. You stay here. I could use some air."

Annie brushed past him anyway. Elijah went to follow but George grabbed his shoulder. He whispered forcefully in Elijah's ear, loud enough for the entire room to hear, "Don't act so high and mighty, you hypocrite. Why else would you be here with a girl you hardly know?"

Elijah jerked his arm free and left, calling after Annie.

A bony finger went up. "I have a theory."

Felicity rose on her long legs. She circled among them like a TV detective working the room. "I think maybe there's a spirit in this house that doesn't like what we're doing... or precisely, *who* we're doing it with. Like maybe we should take a good hard look at who's sleeping with who in this house, because maybe it's not what the universe wants."

Heads jerked up all over the room, each staring at the other in amazement.

George glared, eyes dark with contempt. "Do you pick your moments to be an absolute bitch, or does it just happen spontaneously?"

Felicity looked at her friends, shocked—shocked!—they didn't agree with her. Finding no solace, she stormed from the room, the front door slamming shut behind her.

Gretchen licked her fly-paper lips and smiled with gratitude. She could have kissed George if she didn't fear her face would get stuck to his.

CHAPTER TEN

Elijah's hand was slippery on the gear shift. Annie rode shotgun, clutching her seatbelt with one hand and the door frame with the other as the tiny Beetle lurched forward, stopped, then forward again.

"No. Left up is first gear. Back is second. If you want to go faster, it's right up three, back right four."

Elijah made a short "uh, huh" sound with his throat, completely and utterly confused. He cracked sarcastically, "It's just like riding my ten speed."

Annie's voice was droll and a little impatient. "No, it's completely different."

He drove past Felicity's car, jammed halfway into a hundred-year old oak tree, its radiator still steaming. He jerked and jolted his way off the property, stalling one last time on the gravel road to let Annie out.

They sat in silence for what felt the longest time. Elijah made no eye contact, preferring to stare out the windshield and watch the fog creep in over the lake. Finally, Annie placed her hand over his. Her touch was like bottled lightning. "You sure you don't want me to go with you?"

Elijah nodded. The moon hung low and full in front of him, almost as a warning not to divulge what he was thinking of telling her.

But he had to.

He turned toward Annie and, noting her concerned look, said "I can't do this."

Her face fell. "It's a stick shift, dude, not calculus."

"No, I wasn't talking about the car. I meant about—"

"I know what you meant, Elijah." Annie pulled her hand away. She reached for her door handle to leave, then stopped. "Look, if you're worried about George, don't be. He was just angry. I'm sure he didn't mean any of those things."

But George did, Elijah thought to himself. *He meant every word*. But he couldn't acknowledge that now.

"It's not George. It's..."

He paused, hoping to give what he said next its proper emphasis because it was going to be important. Unfortunately what came out was:

"You see... God has His finger in me."

Annie's brow furrowed. A smile teased at her lips from his awkward word choice.

Elijah quickly realized what he had said and added, panicking, "*On* me! *On* me! He has His finger *on* me. Here.

On my heart. Do you know what I mean?"

She shook her head. "I wish I did, Elijah."

He took a deep breath. "Ever since I was little, as early as I can remember, I was taught God is watching me. So long as I had enough faith in Him, no matter how bad things got, God would be there for me. Everything would work out right... if I behaved. Because when I start to question, have doubts, or stick my head out too far in the wrong direction..."

He slapped his palms together for effect. In his mind's eye, all he could see was a PVC pipe.

His throat seized. He sucked in a huge breath and exhaled. "*I* brought this upon us. It's *my* fault we're being punished like this."

Annie let out a little sigh, as if she was disappointed they were talking about this. "Elijah, what are we being punished *for*? Think about it for a second."

He didn't have to think about it. He knew. Nana had warned him.

She grabbed his hand again. It was warmer this time. "Elijah, I don't believe in a god that would do this. And if God *was* doing this to us, why would anyone believe in someone so cruel?"

He heard the squeak of cheap pleather seat as she pulled closer to him.

"Elijah, it's okay if you're not ready to be... you know... intimate. That's your choice. But ask yourself something...

is it your fear of God that's the problem, or is it that you're afraid of getting close to someone?"

Elijah took a moment. He could barely believe he was here, sitting in Annie's car, talking to her about this. He was more vulnerable and open than he had ever been with anyone his whole life. Now everything in his being told him to retreat. Retreat.

It was always safer to retreat.

"Yes and yes again. Can I say yes to all of that?"

Annie leaned over and kissed Elijah gently on the cheek. He shut his eyes, already regretting his decision, and waited to hear her open the passenger door and step out. As soon as the door shut, he jammed the car in first. The engine grinded like it was being strangled. The car puttered forward, down the gravel road and onto the path through the woods.

Max pushed through the front door to find Felicity on the porch steps crying. He felt a pang of pity for her, even if Felicity most often brought it on herself.

"Seems like you got hit with some shrapnel in there," he said , sitting beside her.

Felicity turned her tear-stained cheeks toward him. "I'm a big girl, Max. I can take it. Not like your little girlfriend in there."

Max nodded. Then, something occurred to him. "You

told George to invite me, didn't you?"

She sniffled. "Maybe."

It suddenly all made sense. He smirked to himself, somewhat flattered and excited by the attention. "You were never good at the just-be-friends shit."

"Whatever happened to us?" Felicity sighed, placing a hand on his thigh.

Something about it felt good. Familiarity, maybe.

"You were crazy," Max said.

"You cheated."

"So did you," he reminded.

"You cheated first."

"Well... you were crazy first."

Felicity leaned her head on his shoulder. Max moved his head slightly, nose against her forehead. The scent of her hair had always been so intoxicating, even if it reminded him of potpourri and wet dog.

She sniffled again. He fumbled around in his pockets, searching for a tissue, a scrap of paper, anything. He found an old receipt for a milkshake in his left pocket and handed it to her. She laughed, but used it anyway. After she wiped her nose, she looked over at him.

"Anything?" she asked, code for booger check.

He smiled and said what he always used to say. "Clean as a whistle."

Felicity leaned her head back on his shoulder, her eyes trained down toward his crotch. "All I want is for a guy to like me. I know I have my days but it's not like I'm some dangerous psycho or anything..." She was grinding her teeth now, the way she did when she was off her meds.

Everything told Max he should run. Instead, his eyes found the tops of her breasts; they were pushed up against her night shirt like two pink balloons wanting to escape into the nighttime sky.

He reconsidered.

Sure, she was a terror most of the time they were dating. The fights, the cheating. But it did lead to some amazing make-up sex. There was something real there, wasn't there? Something real between them? Had he been so consumed with the night's events that he couldn't see what was important? That the person who really, truly cared for him was leaning on his shoulder right this moment?

But what about George? What about his friendship? True, Max never made much effort toward having friends, preferring to just "hang out" with his football and wrestling buddies, but George helped him out of many a scrape with homework, probably through Elijah. George invited him to the cabin out of friendship and here Max was, ready to abandon him. No, he could never betray his only friend.

Felicity crossed her arms in front of her, squeezing her puppies even further out of her shirt.

On second thought, Max reasoned, he could always

find *new* friends.

He cleared his throat before he lifted her chin and stared directly into her big blinking eyes. "There's some crazy shit happening here, Felicity, and I don't know exactly how it's all going to shake loose. But no matter what happens, I got your back. And if I got your back…"

He leaned in closer for the kill.

"… I hope you got mine."

Felicity stared back intently, licking her lips. "Barn?"

Max felt the rise in his boxers. "Five minutes?"

Felicity stood. "Let me wash up."

He would go to Hell for this. He knew it. But he would worry about Hell on Monday.

Annie fiddled with the dials on the radio until she heard a familiar fifties tune. She left it on, lips silently moving to the song's catchy refrain.

George stumbled in from the kitchen, hair rumpled and curly, clutching a wine cooler. "You plugged it back in?"

She shrugged, both hands pressed against the top of the massive old radio. "Too much going on in my head. I just had to hear some music."

He eyed her curiously then grew serious. "Have you seen Felicity?"

"You just missed her storming upstairs."

Rather than follow his girlfriend, George said, "Good."

"I take it your big night didn't go as planned?"

"It did… and it didn't." George plopped on the couch and shrugged, looking up at the second floor bathroom. "I thought I'd feel different, you know? I mean, sure, there's the excitement of being inside another human being, but…"

Annie could see the disappointment in his eyes, as much emotion as he could muster.

"It didn't feel any different than being alone with my laptop and tissue box. I felt like I always feel after I come: empty. Call me crazy, but somehow I thought my first time would be more, I don't know… *romantic*."

Annie drifted from the radio to George. "Tell me about it. Scotty wasn't much of a cuddler."

"Wait… you mean Scotty?… Scotty *Johnson*?"

Annie reached for his wine cooler.

"Give me some of that," she said, taking a sweet, awful swig. She sized him up, hand on hip, foot tapping. Generally she avoided confrontation, but this was a special occasion. "You're a bad friend, you know that? Elijah was really shaken up by what you said."

George simply smiled, dimples on display. "Look, I love the guy, really I do, but…"

Annie usually zoned out whenever anyone had a sentence with a "but" in the middle of it because everything that followed the "but" wasn't worth hearing and never made any difference.

She listened anyway.

"He gets this look on his face, this confused look about how the world works and you just want to slap right off of him. I know I was harsh, but maybe it'll do him so good to question things once in a while. So what if I go through the motions in school? I'm figuring things out, okay? And if that makes me a hypocrite, then, so be it!"

Annie frowned, biting her lip. It tasted like the rest of her mouth, blackberry or whichever hideous flavor the wine cooler was.

George regarded her quietly for a moment. "What I don't get is how Elijah snagged a girl like you."

She turned to the fireplace, grabbed the poker and stoked the dying fire. "Truthfully?"

When she looked up, George was on his feet and slinking toward her. Protectively, she took another sip of the wine cooler.

"Yes, I want to know," he said, sneaking closer. "What's the attraction?"

Annie leaned against the mantel, the fire warm against her backside. "He's *not* a hypocrite. He actually believes. That counts as something."

George nodded, still skeptical. "Uh-huh."

"Plus he's cute. Short. Stout. Like a little teapot. He's not shallow like all the other boys. Like he doesn't think about sex all the time, you know?" She paused, a little buzzed from the cooler. Had it been that long since she'd had a drink? "But… I blew it."

George arched one eyebrow. "What do you mean?"

Annie hanged her head. "I got too slutty. With all that was going on tonight, it seemed like the right thing to do." She chuckled at her own joke and took another swig from his now half-empty cooler. "I came on way too strong. But that's me. Always rushing into burning buildings."

She looked toward the fire, taking another swig too fast. "I used to not speak up when I had feelings. Now I actually tell guys I like them if I do. And each time I get the brush off I wonder what's wrong with me. I mean, why is that? I don't cost that much. I never have a dull line in a conversation. And I know I'm not *that* bad to look at."

George had maneuvered himself right next to her. His eyes looked at her intently under soft lashes, his jaw set in the flickering firelight.

Annie gulped and downed the last of his drink, placing the empty bottle absently on the mantel. "Am I?" she chirped, winding a single lock of copper-red hair around one finger. "You know… bad to look at?"

George cleared his throat. "No. You're not."

She found herself smiling as he inched ever closer. "Well, that clears it. Then something is *definitely* wrong with me!"

His hands caressed her shoulders, gentle but firm. His voice was insistent, his breath sweet from the wine cooler. "There is nothing wrong with you."

Annie blinked twice, trying not to sound so pathetic. "I just wanted him to like me."

Their noses were nearly touching.

"*I* like you."

His kiss was gentle and soft. His hands slipped low around her waist. She melted into his arms, kissing George, seeing Elijah, not sure which she preferred.

Her brain quickly caught up to her hormones. She turned her face to one side, his kiss sloppy on her cheek, and pushed away from him.

"No," she gasped, her throat throbbing, suddenly dizzy. "This is... this is wrong. This is..."

Her stomach clenched and squeezed. She sprinted to the kitchen and proceeded to retch her sticky guts up in the sink.

Fucking wine coolers.

The two headlights of the Beetle pierced the darkness on the lonely mountain road, but their brightness did little to illuminate much beyond five or six feet in front of the bumper.

Elijah's hands gripped the wheel tightly, George's words pounding in his head like a jackhammer, along with his own doubts—those long held, ever-lingering doubts: was God real? What did Elijah know? For sure? Other than what he had been told?

Desperate for distraction, he stole a look in the backseat. It was a mess—schoolbooks with torn covers, binders with torn corners, dirty clothes that looked like they had overflowed from Annie's backpack. The rear dashboard was covered with... plush dolls? Elijah turned back to the road, pondering. He'd never taken Annie for a stuffed animal person.

Then again... what did he really know about her? That she was interested in him, and he had botched it completely, running away scared, from George, from his friends, from Annie, from life?

Elijah sped down the deserted highway, shaking his head, unable to take the noise of his own thoughts another moment longer, when his eyes caught an object on the passenger side floor.

Could it be...?

He pushed on the overhead light to be sure.

Yes. It *was*.

One hand on the wheel, Elijah reached to grab it, stretching his arm to its fullest length. After a few painful seconds, his fingertips seized the prize—a half-open artificially flavored Cherry Chewee Pie.

The exposed part was slightly moldy, looking like the end of a fuzzy slipper; the other half, however, was untouched and—potentially—edible. Heart racing and brow wet in savory anticipation, Elijah turned the pie around in his hand, ready to bite into the non-moldy part.

Soon he would experience the sweet release of the factory-flavored gelatinous goop, rolling it over and over on his tongue as endorphins exploded in his head like fireworks. For a few sugary seconds, he wouldn't have to think about Annie or George or sex or God for that matter...

And he found the whole idea disgusting.

Elijah chucked the Chewee Pie back to the floor and pounded the steering wheel with his fist. "What the hell am I doing?" he cried to the blank windshield. "I'm not hungry—I'm miserable! I'm confused! I should head back, tell Annie I'm sorry and I'm just scared, that's all! *Arrgghh! Fuuuccckkk!!!*"

His Dad's voice came from the backseat. "First sensible thing you've said all evening."

Elijah jerked and looked into the rearview mirror.

His parents were in the backseat, still bloody from the deadly accident that had occurred on that very road. Dad had a jagged piece of glass still sticking from his throat. Mom sat close, her arm looped lovingly through what was left of her husband's sinewy elbow.

"And don't curse in front of your mother."

"Don't be silly," said his mother, nudging her husband's shoulder. "He's getting the girl medication."

His father gurgled through his bloody wounds, "Yeah, but he doesn't have to be an *asshole* about it."

His mother's shriek was high and guttural; nothing ghostly about it. "Allen! My word...!"

"Sorry Myra, but I'm telling the truth. It's about time someone knocked some sense into this kid."

Elijah faced the road, white knuckles on the wheel. First his dead parents came to him in a dream. Then there was the fiery vision of the man in the black suit who watched him get a bedpost planted in his eye socket. Now he was chauffeuring his dead parents as they bickered in the back seat. Was this really happening? Was *any* of this real?

Of course it was real. It was all real. It was too weird not to be.

He decided to roll with it.

Elijah relaxed his grip on the steering wheel. "Mom... was I being... you know, an asshole?" he asked, desperate for a little parental advice, ghostly or otherwise.

His mother leaned forward, blood dripping onto the console between the front seats. "Son, we think it's great you think God is punishing you. It shows good character. But you shouldn't be so hard on yourself."

His father shook his head, which threatened to come loose from the great gash across his throat. "So you lied to Nana. I lied to Nana all the time. And look at me. I turned out fine."

Elijah resisted the temptation to remind his father that he died in a tragic accident in full view of the "Welcome to Devil's Catch" sign. Instead, he asked, "Are you in heaven?"

Dad bristled in his seat. "Does it *look* like we're in

heaven?"

"You mean you're in…?" Elijah hesitated even finishing the question.

It was Mom's turn to be insulted. "What did you think we were in our lifetimes? Heathens?"

"Is there a God?"

In the backseat, his parents exchanged looks. Mom spoke first. "That's not important."

Elijah's head was ready to explode. *Not important*?!?"

"What *is* important," Dad said, "is there's a very pretty girl waiting for you in the cabin. And her heart is breaking."

Mom agreed, in a fashion. "Plus you shouldn't be so choosy. You're not exactly handsome in the traditional sense. And by traditional sense, we mean pleasing to the eye."

Elijah couldn't believe it; his parents had come back to haunt him and all they could think to do was insult him.

"But we love you," his mother added, almost as an afterthought. She nudged her husband's rib, poking out of his shirt.

Dutifully, he nodded. "We love you, son."

Mom sat forward and, offering one last bit of motherly advice, pointed to the road. "And watch out for that guy."

There, in the middle of the highway, stood the man in black, his pale face even more ghostly in the headlights.

Elijah crushed the brakes. Books, jackets, sweaters, lip

gloss and plush dolls went flying. The car screeched to a stop.

When he looked back to the road, the man was gone. A drift of fog floated lazily past the dotted center line.

His parents were gone as well.

Elijah inhaled and exhaled rapidly, as if measured breathing could reassure himself of his sanity. His lap was covered with makeup cases, books and backpacks from Annie's car. He dumped the junk from his lap onto the passenger seat.

A book cover caught his eye, but the inside of the car was so dark it was hard to see. He picked it up, held it to the moonlight and read the title.

The Wiccan Way of Life.

Elijah flipped through the pages and stopped at an illustration of a pentagram—the same pentagram tattooed on the small of Annie's back.

His mouth opened involuntarily. The saliva on his tongue went desert-dry. He scoured the passenger seat to scan the rest of the titles.

They came at him, fast and furious: *Wicca for Dumdums. The Books of Magick: Protection from Spells.*

Elijah found one last book, open to a dog-eared chapter titled "Protection Against Evil Spells."

He gazed into the rearview mirror, hoping his parents might come back. He only saw his panicked reflection as it slowly dawned on him:

"Annie's... a witch?"

Annie, her stomach still queasy, sat in the lotus position in the middle of the kitchen, lights off, surrounded by three flickering votive candles. The house was quiet as Annie began to speak an incantation:

> *"Spirit of light, by my will, I summon you to this place. Cast your favor upon these needles and me. To each needle, grant your power that no evil intrusion may pass, lest it suffer upon it your unyielding retribution."*

From a messenger bag at her side, Annie pulled out a pin cushion. One by one, she stuck five pins inside it and laid the cushion in the center of the candles. Under normal conditions, there would be a bag of lavender beside her and Enya playing the background. But already, she could feel the pins working their magic.

Annie whispered the last incantation:

> *"By my will I call you. By your will, let this be done."*

The votives answered by flickering angrily.

Annie smiled and blew out the candles and hoped she'd gotten the words in the right order this time.

CHAPTER ELEVEN

It took all of her energy not to scream.

Felicity paced back and forth in the upstairs bathroom, frantically rubbing her hands and wrists, murmuring to herself, "I don't know what he sees in that... that... *ginger bitch*!"

She tried to forget the image of George and Annie kissing by the fire but it was burned in her mind as if with acid. George took her all this way to this godforsaken cabin... to what? Humiliate her? If that's the way he was going to disrespect her, then she was going to disrespect him right back!

With steel reserve in her eyes, she faced the bathroom mirror and began to primp herself. She would show George what he missed. Yes, she would be showing him by sleeping with his best friend, but it wasn't about George or Max anymore: it was about *her* and what she wanted.

Finally.

As she applied a second and third layer of lip gloss, a metallic odor wafted into her nostrils. She looked at her reflection.

Blood trickled from her nose.

What the fucker? asked a voice inside her head.

Bloody noses were one of the myriad side effects her doctors warned about when she took her meds, but she hadn't taken any. She ripped a stretch of toilet paper from the holder and wiped her nose until the bleeding stopped.

Running her hands under the water to rinse her face, Felicity looked down to see streams of red swirling the drain. She leaned closer to analyze the substance's thickness and color, more dark than brown. Rusted water? Blood?

Her blood?

She yanked her hands out of the stream. There were no cuts or wounds she could see. Her attention turned back to the water stream. The red stain had surged to a gush.

Blood was bursting from the pipes.

What the fucker is right, agreed a second voice.

Felicity twisted shut both faucet handles and staggered backwards into a towel rack. Trembling, she wiped her hands on a dusty, moth-ridden towel until the nausea in her stomach eased.

A dark red clot soaked through the terry cloth fibers.

She threw the towel across the room and inspected her hands and fingernails. There was nothing to see that was unusual, aside from the hangnail she had been nursing for the past two weeks.

Felicity sat on the edge of the tub to steady her nerves when an alarm tripped her already-frazzled circuits. She opened her legs and dipped her head down.

Blood was seeping through the center of her dyed jeans.

Biting her fist, she fought the urge to yell at her crotch: *Now? Now you decide to host a Red Party at Club Menses?*

Can't stop the flow, her crotch answered.

"SHUT UP!" she cried back. "*I'm* in control here! Not you!"

She tossed her dirty jeans into the moth-eaten hamper and replaced them with her favorite micro-mini skirt. After wrapping a beige-colored towel around her waist just in case, Felicity slid open the second-story window and stuck the first leg out, more determined than ever to see Max, menstrual visit or not.

———————

Max discovered a giant scythe resting in the corner of the barn. The blade was clear enough to see his reflection in it, even in the dim lantern light. As he finger-combed his hair, he recalled the firmness of Felicity's body and wondered how it would feel after all this time. His fingers scraped the bandage Gretchen had applied to the back of his head after the frog storm.

"Won't be needing this no more," he said cockily to his

reflection as he yanked off the bandage. Horniness always trumped healing.

Continuing to comb back there, his fingers slipped inside the wound. Something wet squirmed in there.

Something living.

Max pinched it with his fingers. It wouldn't come willingly. He felt every bit of it struggle as he pulled it out of his hair and let it fall into his hand.

In his palm was a head louse. Wet and plump and sticky to the touch, it writhed blindly, twisting and turning and searching for meat.

After letting out an ear-splitting squeal, Max dropped the parasite to the ground and squashed it with the heel of his boot. The sole treads were smeared with an off-white sludge.

Must have fallen from a beam in the ceiling, he thought. *Maggots love to feast on rotting wood. Right?* Besides, Max kept his hair dandruff free. He was anal about those sorts of things.

It *couldn't* be...

He bent closer to the blade and gave his hair a playful tussle. As his fingers groomed his scalp, something looking like rice fell out. One piece followed by another. And another. And another. The rice landed on the ground.

Max saw they were squiggling.

He gripped the scythe closer to his face. In the scythe's reflection, he saw his head was bristling with lice.

Wriggling, slithering, squirming, raveling lice. Feasting on his flesh.

Max dropped the scythe and ran in circles, scratching at his scalp. Each time he pulled his hand his away his fingers were crawling with lice.

Then he felt an itch. On his groin.

His eyes widened.

No, it couldn't happen. Not to him. Not *now*.

He didn't want to look.

Max took a deep breath, unbuttoned his jeans and yanked open his jockey shorts.

What he saw made him whimper like a little baby.

———————

Gretchen tossed and turned in Nana's old bed. Try as she might, she couldn't sleep for more than a minute at a time. Her head was swimming with too many thoughts.

All of them were about Max.

She would have been sleeping side by side with the star football player that evening if it hadn't had been for her ballooning head. The swelling would go away eventually, she knew; Max's behavior toward her would not. It was already leaving a scar.

Not half an hour earlier he had been inside of her, so close she could taste his eyeballs. She hadn't remembered anything after that. Her girlfriends at school had warned her beforehand, prepping her with tales of how men change after sex; how they become cold and distant once they'd gotten their poison out, even to the point of changing personalities. She knew Max was skittish about certain things—spiders, clowns, unwanted body hair. She couldn't do anything about the first two, but she made darn sure she waxed prior to the weekend. But for Max to accuse her of demonic possession? She couldn't wait to tell the girls about *that* one.

A rustling sound outside caused her to sit up. It was soon followed by a muffled squeal.

Her joints and back aching, Gretchen struggled to stand. Her infection made everything seem surreal and blurry. Still, she slowly hobbled toward the window to see what was going on.

The moon hung low and bright. Below it a tiny light shone from inside the barn. She saw Max's silhouette darting in and out of the glow. It looked like he was dancing.

The bastard!

More squeals came from outside. Closer this time. They seemed to be coming from the window next to hers.

Gretchen pressed her pumpkin-sized head against the glass, unable to see beyond the peripheral, when she saw Holy Ghost High School's cheerleading captain drop from the sky and land squarely on her butt on the ground below.

Fascinated, Gretchen watched Felicity stagger to her

feet, straighten out the towel she'd wrapped around her waist and dash off in the direction of the barn.

The little freshman gnashed her teeth so hard she felt one of her zits pop.

CHAPTER TWELVE

Elijah sat in the car, the questions in his brain revolving faster than the engine.

He had flipped through *The Books of Magick*, a maddening collection of rites and rituals, diagrams and pentacles, signs and symbols and... menstrual cycles? Did people actually read this stuff? Did Annie?

The most nagging question settled low in his gut: was Annie responsible for everything that had happened that night?

Elijah gazed up at the moon, his eyes pleading for answers, when an object brushed against the driver door, heavy enough to jiggle a one-ton vehicle.

In the driver's side mirror, looking much closer than it appeared, was the wolf. From the unusual markings on its snout, Elijah knew it was the same wolf he'd seen driving up to the cabin. The creature rubbed its scent along the front quarter-panel and stopped in the middle of the road, bathed in the headlights of Annie's car.

Elijah blasted the horn.

The wolf refused to give any ground.

He tried the horn twice. A third time.

The wolf glared at him, teeth bared, its yellow eyes ablaze in the car's halogen light.

Determined he would force the wolf out of his way one way or another, Elijah reached for the clutch with his foot and grabbed the gear shift and...

The engine stalled. Annie's VW Beetle shuddered and shimmied to a stop.

Terrific.

Elijah turned the ignition key. The engine started and static punctured his eardrums. The car radio switched on—switched itself on?—and the all too familiar voice filled the inside of the car:

> *"The Lord sent me to you with the message: 'Let my people go to worship me in the desert.' But as yet you have not listened... If you refuse to let my people go, I warn you, tomorrow I will bring loc—"*

His fingers couldn't fly fast enough to turn it off.

For a moment, Elijah relished the silence, he and the wolf, when he heard a rumble in the distance. He rolled down the window a smidge to better hear.

No, it wasn't a rumble, it was more like a... *buzz*. Faint

but detectable. Whatever it was, it wasn't a stationary sound.

And it was getting louder.

Within seconds, the air around the car pulsed. Vibrations shook the floorboards and seat. A tremor crawled up Elijah's spine as he rolled the window back up tight.

The buzzing took on a physical presence. Tree branches cracked. Bark shredded from trunks. Even the wolf was scared. Its head darted from one side of the road to the other, back arched, poised to attack whatever was to come from the bushes.

And suddenly it sprang, clearing the nearby trees: a massive, moving black cloud. In one fell swoop it descended upon the wolf. The wolf tried to fight back, its teeth snapping impotently against the cloud, white foam dripping from its mouth. It was to no avail. The cloud seized the creature like a giant, angry fist and lifted it off the ground. The twin beams of the Beetle's headlights gleamed onto a now-empty road as the wolf's final painful whimper echoed in the moonlit sky.

Elijah, slack-jawed and doe-eyed, sat frozen to his seat, unable to process what he had just seen.

He hadn't seen anything yet.

Clumps of fur rained down upon the road, wet and sticky, piling up until there was a mass of flesh and bone where the wolf once sat. The wolf's jawbone clattered to the asphalt next to the pile, picked clean.

Elijah, his rapid pulse beating against his eardrums, knew he was next.

Careful not to make any sudden movements, Elijah pressed his foot on the clutch and gently shifted the car into neutral. Quietly and delicately, he reached for the key...

The buzzing came back. This time the noise was as loud on the inside as it was on the outside. Elijah frantically turned the ignition. By some miracle the car jittered to life and, after a few false starts, launched forward.

The cloud was before him, blackening the road and swallowing up the moon. Elijah steered the car into a clumsy U-turn before flooring the gas, racing the tiny Beetle as fast as it could go, the bottom of his sneaker flush with the floor. He peered in the rear view. The cloud was right behind him, shearing off tree limbs and clobbering small shrubs in its path.

It appeared to be *gaining* on him.

"What was it again? Up three? Down four?" He lost speed to the steep mountain terrain. Blackness engulfed his rear view mirror, a giant, buzzing black cloud, of what he had no earthly—or unearthly—idea.

Elijah stripped the last of Annie's gears. "Come on! Up four!" He ratcheted the clutch as far as it would go and wedged it into place. At last, the engine's full revolutions kicked in. The car surged forward, giving Elijah some distance from the deadly menace. The buzzing diminished to a low hum until finally it died altogether. He checked the mirror to be sure.

Nothing was behind him except brake lights.

Exhaling a huge sigh of relief, Elijah turned back to the mountain road.

The word REPENT filled the windshield.

Elijah blindly spun the steering wheel but too late: glass rained upon him as the hood smashed into the wooden sign and the car crumpled to a violent halt. Steam gushed from the engine in the back compartment and filled the inside of the car.

Dazed with fumes, Elijah lifted the driver's side handle only to find his door wedged against a tree. He shoved against the door, thrusting with his shoulder, desperate to get out, when he felt the ground shake like a low-magnitude earthquake.

The cloud was coming.

Elijah frantically rolled down the window and squeezed his fat body out of the car. He stood on his feet, slightly dizzy but coherent enough to recognize the buzzing cloud was advancing closer by the second. He hop-limped the remaining quarter-mile to the cabin, not knowing which he feared more: confronting Annie about her witch books or having his own jawbone picked clean.

CHAPTER THIRTEEN

Felicity creaked open the barn door and peeked her head inside. "Maxie?"

The single oil lantern cast dark shadows all around the barn. There was movement in one of the shadows. Squinting, Felicity could see Max with his back to her.

He was tying something to his head.

"Maxie, baby?" she called out, sliding the door shut behind her.

The football star stepped out of the black. He was wearing a doo-rag fashioned from a torn piece of his shirt. Of all the looks Max could sport, Felicity never once thought he'd go for gangsta.

"My," Felicity chuckled, advancing to him. "Aren't we retro?"

She slid into his arms. He felt so good and warm, his lips so tempting in the warm light.

"What's with the towel, hun?" he asked.

"Never mind that," Felicity said, drawing him closer. "Kiss me."

His lips were soft and exploring against hers. His hands began slow, intimate circles at the small of her back. Her knees weakened. His tongue probed so deep inside her mouth, she gasped for oxygen. They tumbled backwards onto a haystack, lips still locked.

Her desire mounting, Felicity reached underneath his shirt, desperately wanting to touch his rock hard body again.

Max clutched her hands and pushed her away. "Let's take it nice and slow."

That was a first.

"What's gotten into you?" she asked, breathless.

Sweat was forming on his brow. "Er... it's nothing. Nothing." Max kissed her again, long and hard. His hands gripped the side of her hips as he pressed his arousal against the towel.

Felicity pulled back, mindful she had to keep a safe distance between their crotches.

"What's with *you*?" he asked, scratching his head. "Usually you can't wait to get started."

She didn't want to tell him that she was feeling a lot of activity down there, especially since she wasn't completely sure what *kind* of activity. She stood and backed away a few feet and tightened the towel around her waist. "It's nothing, nothing," was all she could think to say.

There was only one way to satisfy Max and keep him from finding out she was a bleeding gusher of gross. She searched for the deepest, blackest corner she could find and knelt down inside of it.

"Come here," she beckoned from complete darkness.

Max joined her.

Going only by touch, Felicity lifted up his shirt and peppered his torso with tiny kisses. He leaned back and moaned.

That's my baby.

She undid his top button and slid her hand into the waistband of his boxer briefs and felt something... crunchy.

"Babe," Felicity asked, "have you been eating in your boxers again?"

"No. Why?"

"Because it feels like you got Chinese food all over your lap."

Max yelped, pulled his pants up and backed away several feet.

"You don't like it, baby?" Felicity asked, sitting back.

Max shook his head. He was really sweating now, stumbling over his words. "No, no, no, no, no, no... I-I'm f-f-fine, baby... just fine..."

Seeing him in the light, Felicity swore she saw something move underneath his doo rag. She quickly threw the thought away.

"Let's do something else," Max suggested.

She rocked back on her heels, licking her lips coyly. "Okay. Like what?"

"Let me go down on you." He went for her towel.

It was Felicity's turn to leap away. "Noooooo, no!" she insisted. "Let me go down on *you*..."

She reached for his pants.

Max skidded away from her. "No, no, no! Not such a good idea, hun."

"Well," Felicity exhaled, assessing the situation, "what do we do now?"

Max scratched his head again. "Wanna play cards?"

The barn doors flew open.

Felicity and Max jumped.

Gretchen stood at the entrance, quiver on her back, a bow held firm in her outstretched arm. Her face was bloated and round, orange bordering on red, her mouth and eyes little more than slits. Felicity couldn't tell if her eyes were leaking pus or tears when the tiny freshman slid an arrow from the quiver, positioned it on the string... and aimed it directly at Max's crotch.

"I GAVE YOU MY V-CARD!" she shouted.

Max picked up the closest weapon he could find—a shovel—and positioned the blade defensively in front of his pelvis. "Gretchen... honey, *sweetie*... put the bow and arrow down."

Gretchen sneered. "I had a hookup list. Did you know

that? Tom was my number three. But he wouldn't cut his hair..."

WHOOSH!

Felicity screamed as Gretchen fired an arrow just above Max's head. The arrow stuck in the wall and throbbed.

Gretchen loaded another arrow. "Brian, all-star varsity, was my number four. We were in a locker room together. He finger-banged me. Do you know how hard it is not to go beyond a *finger-banging*?"

Felicity stepped in to do her best damage control, though it was hard to look at the chick's scab-riddled face without cringing. "Gretchen, we didn't do anything. He didn't want to–"

WHOOSH!

The arrow shot past Felicity's head, so close to her ear she felt the feather scratch her lobe on its way past. It slammed into the wall behind her with a *thwoinggg*.

Felicity touched her ear to make sure it was still there. When she pulled her finger back, she saw blood.

Bitch!

Gretchen reached for another arrow and crept toward Max. "Justin, number six... I would have let him eat me out. Ronnie, number seven... a blowjob. Adrian, number eight... a finger-bang, maybe a titty fuck..."

Max, hands trembling, near tears, pleaded for his life— and his manhood. "Put it down, Gretchen. Just... put it down!"

Felicity added, "Yeah, Gretchen, just—"

Gretchen turned to her with a growl.

The sight of her face made Felicity's voice stall in her throat.

Gretchen whipped her giant face back toward Max. "But you... *you* were my number one. I gave you my V-card willingly. Heck, I would have even given you my *A*-card!... but now it's too late... IT'S ALL TOO LATE!"

Gretchen tightened her stance and squeezed her left eye shut. Felicity scooped up a mound of dirt and flung it at Gretchen's wretched face. Blinded, Gretchen let go of the arrow.

WHOOSH!

The arrow sank into a nearby hay bale.

Felicity grabbed Max's hand and lugged him through the barn doors. The two fled into the woods, the shovel gripped tightly in Max's hand.

Another WHOOSH sounded beside them. A fresh arrow stabbed a nearby tree.

Felicity sped faster.

They ran into a thicket of trees, breathless, aimless, the moon barely able to penetrate the brush as they stumbled along, hand in hand. When Felicity's lungs threatened a mutiny, she tugged at Max's grasp to stop. They paused under a gnarled oak to catch their breath, holding each other and shivering.

"Which... which way should we go?" Max panted.

Felicity shrugged and nuzzled against Max's broad shoulders. He was in her arms. Even in the face of impending death, this was her victory. And she was going to declare it.

"I don't care, Max, so long as you're near me. Just promise me you'll never leave me again."

WHOOSH!

WHOOSH!

WHOOSH!

Three arrows imbedded in a nearby tree no more than six inches from Max's head.

Max untangled himself from Felicity's arms, grabbed his shovel and sprinted toward the nearest group of trees faster than she had ever seen him run on a Friday night football field.

CHAPTER FOURTEEN

George was the first to hear Max's screams.

He sprinted from the porch and bolted in the direction of the sound. He was surprised to notice Annie was close behind him. Together they raced through the woods, branches slapping them in the face.

They found Max cowering behind a tree, desperately clinging to a shovel.

George asked straight out, "Dude, what's wrong?"

Max looked up, eyes rimmed white, sweat dripping from his forehead. He shook his head, hands clutched to the shovel, as if the garden tool was the only thing keeping him sane.

Behind him, a twig snapped. "Get down," Max whimpered, reaching for them both.

George wasn't alarmed until he felt a gust of wind against his cheek and heard the *piiing* of an arrow ricochet off the shovel in Max's hand.

"Holy shit!" said Annie, scrambling for cover.

George hit the ground. Wet earth filled his nostrils.

Footsteps approached. A pair of tiny white sneakers came into George's line of vision. Glancing up, he saw Gretchen—or someone he *assumed* was Gretchen. The swelling had completely distorted her appearance. Her eyes were now slits, thin as coin slots, her mouth puckered like a balloon knot. She slid an arrow into her bow.

Max got up, blathering, both hands on the handle of the shovel. "Gretchen, honey, darling... I know I did you wrong... I see that now... I know I can treat you better... so I've been thinkin'... what do you think... of you and me... going steady?"

She cocked her elbow back.

Max took off.

Gretchen aimed the arrow straight at Max's retreating back when a chastising voice from the dark shouted at her.

"GRETCHEN, HOW COULD YOU!"

The deformed freshman whipped around, head cocked, arrow at the ready. She scanned the dense forest in front of her.

Felicity emerged from behind a tree. George had seen Felicity look a wreck before, usually when someone said "no" to her, but never to this extent: snot ran from her nose, mascara stained her cheek. Still, her stance was defiant.

"Really Gretchen, how could you?" Felicity's voice was

hoarse from crying, desperate from begging. "I thought... I thought we were going to be *best friends*."

"Fuck you, bitch," Gretchen sneered. Her taut fingers pulled back the string, the arrow aimed straight at the center of Felicity's forehead.

George wanted to shut his eyes but he couldn't—Max was creeping silently behind Gretchen, shovel raised above his head, baseball-style, ready to swing.

There was no way he was going to miss *this*.

George watched with baited breath as the bowstring creaked, the shovel rose high in the air, and—

Elijah burst through the foliage. "Guys-guys-we-hafta—"

Gretchen spun toward Elijah and released the arrow. It sank into the trunk right next to Elijah.

Max swung the shovel.

A wet, suckling human-tissue noise preceded the ugly clang of metal against bone as Gretchen's face dislodged from her head. The group silently witnessed the skin, mask-like and rubbery, slide off the shovel's tip and flop to the ground, the fleshly remains of her dainty cheekbones and girlish smile now resembling nothing more than a deflated tire.

The rest of Gretchen stood in shock, eyes bulged and unable to blink, teeth missing, air bubbling out through her nose-less cartilage. She dropped the bow. Her fingertips leapt upward to her throat, past her exposed chin and along her creaking jawbones, her skull shining white in the moonlight. She gasped a final breath before muttering, "*Maxxsshh,*" and collapsed to the ground.

Max danced a bizarre holy-shit-what-have-I-done tribal dance, his panic rising in tongues from his vocal chords as everyone else turned away, retching, crying, trembling, screaming, freaking out all at once.

Elijah screamed, "Max, what the hell did you do that for!"

Felicity screeched at him, eyes wide with rage. "Gretchen was going to kill me! Max saved my life!"

Max knelt down and poked Gretchen's lifeless body with one tentative finger. He looked up at Felicity and snapped, "I was gonna *hit* her, not *KILL* her! Then all of the sudden Elijah ran up." He shifted his anger to the little guy. "Look, Elijah! Look what you made me do!"

"I had something to tell you guys!" Elijah yelled back, his face drained of all color.

Annie made a beeline to Elijah and clasped his arm. "Elijah, what were you going to tell us?"

Elijah jumped at her touch. He yanked his arm away, only to have it shaken by George.

"Tell us what, Elijah?" George barked. "WHAT?"

His buddy stammered, trying to hide his panic. "Th-th-they're coming."

George, in no mood for riddles, gripped his friend's shoulders. "*Who's* coming, Elijah?"

Elijah pointed up in reply, his eyes on the trees.

The tree directly above them came alive with buzzing. Creaking, cracking, buzzing, more buzzing, leaves falling, hitting the ground. Branches bowed under the weight of something invisible. Left, right, just above, higher still, the trees swayed and moaned as, just as suddenly, the buzz died down and turned to silence.

The group stood still. Very still.

George whispered, "Don't... anyone... move."

Elijah nodded, and, almost subconsciously, made a step toward him.

His sneaker landed on a twig and snapped it in two.

For a second, nothing happened. George thought maybe, just maybe, they would all steal away to safety.

And all of the sudden the locusts were everywhere. Great, big, crackling locusts, flying between them, around them, into them, landing on the ground, carpeting the ground, filling the air so they couldn't breathe or move. Even Annie, not two feet away, was too far to reach through the cloud of wings and insect legs.

George waved his hands madly. Their skin was like armor, battling his face, his hands, his neck, anywhere his skin lay exposed. They were in his shirt, his hair, everywhere. They crawled, they clung, they flew, they buzzed, buzz, buzz, buzz. He tried to scream but as soon as he opened his mouth they crept inside, filling his mouth, crawling into his nose.

Chewing through the tough locust skin and spitting out their crinkling wings, George cried out, "The cabin!" They followed him, the blind leading the blind, lost amidst the immense chirping, buzzing cloud. It was like being in a tunnel, a moving tunnel, with all the light blacked out. George could see the cabin in sight, its flickering porch light covered by what looked like to be a million locusts. He shielded his face with his arms and sprung onto the porch steps, taking them two at a time. Finally making it inside, George slammed the door behind him.

Elijah yanked on the door handle five, ten, a dozen times.

It was locked.

"Let us in!" Elijah screamed. With a mouthful of locusts, it came out more like, "*Accck uuut iiiiiin.*"

Annie joined him, pounding on the door with one hand and swatting the thick cloud of locusts with the other. "Let us in you creep! These things are going to eat us alive!"

Through the window, Elijah saw George inside, stumbling around, waving a throw pillow at the few dozen locusts that had followed him inside.

Elijah couldn't think; he could barely see.

Annie had already taken off her sweater. Wrapping it around her fist, she punched the glass window, shattering it into a million tiny pieces. She stuck her hand through the broken window and unlocked the door. She threw open the door and pulled him inside.

Elijah shut the door behind them but the cloud of locusts poured in through the broken window like thick, black oil out of a just-opened can. George spun around by the fire, frantically brushing off the teams of locusts gathered on his shoulders and neck.

Elijah cried, "Oh my God, George—your back!"

George caught his reflection by a mirror. Perched upon George's back, clinging to his shirt, was a locust the size of a great lobster, with antenna nearly a foot long and legs the size of snow crabs.

Elijah watched his old friend lose it.

Raising his hands and flailing them in the air, George shot up the stairs, shaking and wriggling his shoulders in a vain attempt to loosen the locust-lobster's grip on his back.

Annie grasped Elijah by the hand and shoved him into the kitchen. She pushed the kitchen door shut. Here, at least, was a respite from the buzzing, save for the steady drumming of locusts beating against the windows.

It didn't last.

Elijah pointed at the floor. "Look at your feet!"

Dozens of locusts crawled in under the two-inch gap between the bottom of the door and the kitchen floor.

"Damn," Annie cursed.

Elijah knelt beside Annie and helped her wedge a dusty old apron into the gap, but the persistent locusts swarmed around their fingers and crawled over their hands and arms. Giving up, they flattened themselves against the far kitchen wall and watched as, wing by wing, claw by claw, the locusts squeezed under the door and flew right for them.

Elijah peered over Annie's shoulder out the window. Outside Max and Felicity were covered in locusts from head to toe like a pair of beekeepers. The bugs tore away Felicity's blouse and Max's shirt. The two stumbled about, dazed, half-naked, struggling to find each other and then being torn apart by another massive wave of flying projectiles.

It looked like a horrible way to die.

Elijah turned away. Locusts were squirming in Annie's hair as she beat them off, hands and fingers bloody. The end would come for them soon.

"I know what you are!" Elijah shouted above the growing din.

Annie swatted away a locust that was trying to crawl into her ear. "What?"

Elijah pulled her close to him so tightly the locusts could barely crawl between them. He looked her straight in the eyes and yelled, "I KNOW WHO YOU ARE!"

Her face wore an odd, challenging expression. "What am I?"

"You're a witch!"

Her eyes grew big and wide as if she was reminded she had left a loaf in the oven. "Oh. Good idea!"

Annie quickly removed a piece of black chalk and drew a circle on the floor, pushing away locusts as she closed it. She crawled inside the center of the circle and crossed her legs.

"What are you doing?" he asked.

She held a "shush" finger up and, spitting out a few locusts, replied, "Praying."

Elijah then watched Annie—the perfect stranger he invited to spend a weekend with him at Devil's Catch—lower her head, close her eyes and begin to chant:

> *"From whence they came return them now. Evil that has traveled near, I call on you to disappear. Elementals hear my call. Remove these creatures from these walls."*

She repeated the chant, her voice growing deeper, until the words streamed out in a gurgling croak:

> *"Remove these creatures from these walls and outside, remove these creatures from these walls and outside, remove these creatures from these walls and outside..."*

Elijah backed away, fearing Annie's odd new voice and the way her eyeballs fluttered wildly beneath her closed lids.

He had to get out of there.

He waved his numb hands, barely feeling the locusts

eating his flesh, and swatted a path through the growing cloud of locusts until he reached the kitchen door, now so weighed with insects it appeared bent in the middle. He gripped the door handle.

Warm, wet liquid seeped through his fingers.

Elijah looked down. His hand was covered with green and yellow guts, made more appalling by the brittle pieces of locust shell he had just crushed.

He felt a scream coming on.

Then a shower of locusts rained down on him, followed by a veil of absolute silence. Elijah glanced around at his feet.

The locusts in the kitchen were dead.

Annie stepped out the circle and smacked her hands together to dust away chalk residue.

She smiled.

Scared of her even more, Elijah pushed open the kitchen door to escape. A sea of dead locust husks, enough to cover nearly every inch of the hardwood floor, lay scattered around the living room before him.

The upstairs door flew open and George ran out, flinging dead locusts from his hair and racing down the stairs.

"Did you see?" he screamed, eyes wild. "Did you see? They're dead! All of them! We're saved—"

George's foot slipped on a pile of husks. He flew over the last three steps and landed hard on his left leg. Elijah winced as the bone snap reverberated throughout the cabin, followed by George's tearful screams of pain.

The door swung open. Max walked in, tears streaking down his cheeks. He carried Felicity's half-naked body in his arms. Her head was lolled to the side, her eyes pale and lifeless. Max gently set Felicity on the floor, her body crunching the deceased locusts like a boot stomping on a pile of dead leaves.

"Guys," Max said, sniffling, "I think… she's…"

Elijah stood like a statue amidst the appalling screams and blubbering wails. His eyes bounced from Annie, who was now helping dress George's leg, to Max, who was hunched over the body of Felicity, to the open front door through which he could escape this nightmare. He started for the direction of the door when Max shouted, "LOOK!"

Felicity's face vibrated.

Everyone in the room stopped what they were doing. Even George stopped screaming.

Max knelt closer. "Felicity?"

Her teeth chattered in response.

Max reached his hand out to touch her cheek when a fat, wet locust squeezed out of Felicity's mouth and plunked to the floor, lifeless. Felicity's eyes popped open as she sat up and let out a terrifying banshee-like scream.

Elijah and the rest covered their ears, waiting for the scream to die out. When it finally did, Felicity panted breathlessly and took in her surroundings.

Her eyes met Elijah's.

"Are we dead yet?" she asked.

Out the front door Elijah saw Gretchen's lifeless, faceless body on the ground.

"No, Felicity... We're not dead..."

Then he looked at Annie.

"Not yet anyway."

CHAPTER FIFTEEN

"I'm not a witch. I'm a Wiccan."

Annie swept the last of the dead locusts into the pan and tossed the debris into the fireplace. She was used to resistance her new found calling; in fact, she expected it. She explained herself several times to the group, but they just didn't get it.

Elijah was having the hardest time. "So you mean, like, you worship Satan?" he asked, his eyebrows raised in complete puzzlement.

"No. I told you, Wiccans don't believe in Satan." She watched the locusts' husks crack and sizzle in the fire. They turned into a green, acrid smoke that disappeared up the chimney.

"But what about that thing? That devil symbol on your butt?"

Annie wished she had a dollar for every time she had to answer that question. "That's my pentacle. And it's a *magickal* symbol, not Satanic, thank you very much. Wiccans don't believe in evil any more than you believe in the Easter Bunny."

Elijah shook his head. "But I... I saw you. You were doing a spell."

She clucked her tongue, leaning on the broom. "Yeah. A *protection* spell. In light of everything that was going on, I thought it was a good idea."

George shifted on the sofa, his leg propped up and held in place by a crude splint. "Protection against what?"

Annie narrowed her eyes and glanced around the disheveled cabin. "Hello! Do any of you still think what's happening to us is *natural*? Something or someone is doing this to us. There's a dark energy at work here, people."

Max paced behind George. He wore one of Elijah's ridiculously small shirts, which exposed half his waist and both armpits. He stopped his pacing to ask, "What energy? You mean, like a demon?"

Annie rested against the broom heavily, suddenly bone-weary. "No. Not a demon. You see, Wiccans don't really believe in that either..."

"Well, what *is* it?" Elijah said, his voice rising an octave.

Annie took a deep breath. This was going to be a doozy: "I believe there's a spiritual presence here, born out of intense emotion and energy. Our activities must have set it free. Now it's manifested itself somehow and it's sending us plagues because it wants us to leave. I felt it when I first arrived."

Elijah freaked. "*What*! W-why didn't you say so?"

"I didn't want to be impolite." Annie lowered her voice for sarcastic effect. "'*Thank you for inviting me here and oh by the way there's an evil energy in your house.*'"

Felicity lay sideways in the wing chair, covered in several blankets. It was almost painful to watch her slow, lizard-like brain try to make sense of it all. "So what you're saying is... you can you create fireballs and stuff?"

"No! I'm a Wiccan. *Wiccan.*" Exasperated, Annie tossed aside the broom. "Don't let the broom fool you!"

George struggled into a sitting position. "So... *you're* not doing this to us?"

"That would be against my creed, the Rule of Three."

Her answer met with puzzled faces.

"The Law of Return," she explained.

No comprehension.

She tried a quote. "'*Whatever energy a person puts out into the world will be returned to that person threefold.*'"

More blank faces.

She tried a t-shirt slogan. "*Karma's a bitch*?"

Finally, they all nodded in unison.

Elijah, glancing at the radio, turned to her, his voice nearly pleading, "If what you're saying is true... how do we stop it?"

She gave him the only answer she knew: "We can't."

His face dropped. "But-but... I saw you! You prayed

and chanted and, boom, no more locusts."

Annie shrugged. "That may have been a coincidence. That's the tricky thing with faith. Besides, I'm kinda new at this spell thing."

Elijah grew paler and paler. "You mean we do… *nothing*?"

Annie shook her head. "Spirits can't hurt us. They can only persuade. They set us up, lean back and let us decide what to do. Sorta like what your God does."

"*My* God?" Elijah was having a spasm, spitting his words one at a time. "There…. is… only… *one*… God!" Then he added, as if suddenly needing reassurance, "Isn't there?"

She bit her tongue.

Elijah threw up his hands. "Don't tell me you don't believe in Him either!"

Annie was quick to correct him. "Her."

He turned his back on her.

"Elijah, I know this a lot to take in, but I need to know if you're all right with this." She cupped his hand. "*Are you all right with this*?"

Elijah slowly withdrew his hand from hers and crossed to the other side of the room.

Her heart did a little tumble.

Max stomped forward. "Guys, what's to decide? I don't care if it's God, the Devil, or the Wickedest Witch of the West. You say the spirits don't want us here? I say fine. We leave."

George adjusted his knee on the sofa, wincing from the pain. "How? On foot? Both cars are gone."

Annie knew the answer, although it pained her to say it. "Spirits are most powerful at night. We have to wait until daylight. When morning comes, we hike back, find the nearest policeman, and hope for the best."

They looked at her as if she had just told them they had to repeat a school year.

"So we stay here until another one of us dies?" Max blurted impatiently.

Annie took over the center of the room, not exactly craving the spotlight but desperate to make some sense of the situation. "You're not getting it, people! No one has to die!"

Max pointed at the door. "Gretchen is lying out there in a pool of her own blood! And you're telling us spirits can't hurt us? I don't know about you, Witchiepoo, but those locusts were real."

Annie yelled at the top her voice. "So is *FEAR*! So is *SELFISHNESS*! So is *JEALOUSY*!"

Everyone blinked back their surprise.

"Spirits are sending us the plagues but they can't kill us," Annie continued. "We just have to wait it out and..."

She couldn't believe she had to throw this in, but did.

"...*try not to kill each other before morning.*"

The group was shamed to silence. For the longest while,

no one would make eye contact with the other.

Then a voice spoke out. "Annie's right."

Felicity righted herself in her blanket pile and addressed the group. "Spirits didn't kill Gretchen. Max did. With a shovel. We all saw it."

Max seethed with rage.

Felicity patted his arm. "But that's okay, baby. It was self-defense. We'll back you up in court."

Max whipped his arm away and pounded both fists on the coffee table. "It's YOUR fault this happened! If you hadn't come on to me, Gretchen would still be alive, you selfish bitch!"

"Come on to you?" Felicity barked. "You wanted me. You said you weren't over me."

His face was inches from hers. "You listen to me and you listen good. I don't ever want to hear from you again. I don't want ever to see you again. I'M DONE WITH YOU. DO YOU UNDERSTAND?"

"Don't say that, Max. You don't want that."

"Why the hell not?"

"Because then, dear, you'll be the loneliest inmate in prison."

That was it. Max lunged at Felicity, his hands around her neck. He lifted her from the chair and pinned her to the wall.

"Max! Stop it!" George hobbled across the room and leapt onto his back. He managed to get his arms around

Max's neck, but Max bucked and jerked like a wild bull to throw him off, his hands clamped tight around Felicity's throat.

Elijah stood by the radio.

Annie shouted at him. "Elijah! What are you doing? Help them!"

Elijah timidly approached the buckling bronco that was Max when Annie noticed the radio was glowing with intensity, as if its energy was powered by the very loudness of the room.

Elijah, halfway between his friends and the radio, noticed this too. He stared deeply into the magic eye. The magic eye held him in place as the voice of that archaic reverend spoke appeared to speak directly to him:

> *"Then the Lord said to Moses, 'Stretch out your hand toward the sky so that darkness spreads over Egypt, darkness that can be felt...'"*

"Elijah?" Annie shouted.

His gaze did not break.

Felicity's face turned blue.

Annie screamed at him. "ELIJAH! DO SOMETHING!"

Elijah finally blinked. "Yeah, of course, yeah."

He raced past George and Annie and flew straight out onto the porch, the front door slamming behind him.

Annie cried after him, "Elijah! Where are you going!?!"

But he was gone.

Annie let out a sigh, half out of frustration and half from pity, and rolled up her sleeves.

If you want to do something right...

She joined George. Together they tried to wrench Max's hands free of Felicity's throat, but Max's arms were like pistons, his flesh like steel. Felicity hung limp like a rag doll between his hands, her eyes fluttering and rolling into the back of her head. Annie was waiting, just waiting, for the final vicious snap of her neck... when Elijah burst back in, holding an axe almost as tall as he was.

Annie and George both looked at each other, eyes wide with disbelief, then back at Elijah.

George stammered, "W-w-whoa, there, Elijah. Let's not get crazy here."

Elijah sped across the room, lifted the axe high, and brought it down—

Right on top of the antique radio.

The radio exploded in a burst of electric sparks.

Max loosened his grip on Felicity.

Elijah heaved the giant axe back into the air and brought it down on the radio again and again, rapidly reducing the mahogany console to pieces. The control panel display light blinked on and off. Still, the reverend's voice rang out:

"... No one could see anyone else or move about for three

days..."

Elijah finally reached the guts of the radio, a baffling engine of wires and glass tubes. He sank his axe into it. The radio tubes exploded one by one.

Annie and George succeeded in pulling Max away. Max collapsed to the floor, crying at the ceiling, all the fight gone from him. Felicity slid against the wall, coughing and sputtering for air, her fingers clutching at her throat.

At last the Reverend shut up.

Elijah dropped the axe where it joined the trashed remains of the old radio.

A tiny vacuum tube rolled to his foot. It was the magic eye. Separated from its source, it continued to glow, defiant, desperate, stubborn.

Elijah lifted his foot and drove the heel of his sneaker against it. The tube made a soft *pop* and disintegrated underneath his foot.

At the same time, the hearth went out, the electricity went dead, and the entire cabin plunged into darkness.

"Great," was all someone could think to say.

It was Annie.

CHAPTER SIXTEEN

Felicity rocked back and forth on the old wooden chair in Nana's bedroom. Every back and forth, to and fro movement brought her more in contact with the frigid air. It had been a mild, gentle fall night before; now it felt like the dead of winter.

She hugged her legs close to her chest for warmth and stared, unblinking, at a patch of moonlight on the wall. She would not close her eyes. Not if she could help it. To close her eyes meant reliving the moments when Max was on top of her, hands gripped around her throat. She had expected to see her life pass in front of her eyes.

She didn't see shit.

All she saw was Max, his wretched face contorted in anger, sweat bursting out of his skin, eyes ablaze with hate. *That* was what flashed before her, not her life, not her tournaments, not her trophies, not her parents when they were happy and living under the same roof. None of those highlights came to her. It was as if she never experienced them, or as if they never existed at all.

She did not know what brought her here, to this point; she did not know why she had brutally attacked or why it was suddenly December when it was just October a few minutes ago.

She did know one thing.

This was no way to treat a duchess.

True, she had her days of being a she-bitch of enormous proportions. She owned that. And yes, technically she did try to sleep with her ex under the noses of her current beau and his current... what do you call it, beau-ette? But did she deserve locusts for that? Did she deserve to taste her own windpipe for that? Did she deserve to be alone in a putrid airless room and suffer the plagues of Egypt... for *Max*??

Oh, hell no.

This was all a trick, a trick to set up and humiliate Felicity.

Why?

You don't need reasons, she heard one of her voices say. *The generous people, the people who give without receiving, the ones who are deemed beautiful, always should expect to be misunderstood and scorned for their goodness.*

Felicity agreed, for she considered herself nothing if not misunderstood.

And here she was, the beacon of Holy Ghost High,

treated like an outcast, an idiot with no say, just another dumb blonde.

A second voice chimed in. *Let's bring the bimbo to a haunted house so we can make her our sacrifice and get the hell out of here.*

That was it! The secret of the house. It wanted blood. Heck, it had taken hers. In quarts. Thankfully, the bleeding had stopped a while ago, but as far as she knew she could still be bleeding out of her pants and sticking to the seat. It wasn't morning for a few more hours. There was still time to make her their sacrifice before dawn.

That's what they were doing downstairs. They were discussing how best to kill her.

"Don't kill me! Kill Max! He's the one who deserves it!"

A tiny voice called out into the room. "What did you say?"

Annie was at the door. Or so Felicity presumed. It was hard to separate darkness from darkness. "Felicity, were you talking to yourself?"

Felicity made a half-hearted attempt to speak. To her surprise it came out like a croak. *"Norrrhiiwuzznit."*

Annie's footsteps shuffled inside the room. Felicity curled herself even tighter on the rocking chair and braced for another potential surprise attack.

"Yes, you were," the little witch said. "I heard you. You said something like... 'Kill Max'."

Annie felt her way to the rocking chair. Her hands

found Felicity's shoulders and fumbled up to her face. She pressed a cold palm against her forehead.

"You're burning up," Annie said.

"*Norrrhiimmot.... hiimmcawld,*" Felicity muttered. She felt Max's hands around her throat with every swallow. His hand prints would be on her neck for at least a month.

"We're trying to get the lights back on in the house. Can I get you anything? Water? A warm soda?"

Felicity looked toward the window and shivered. The moon hovered near the cabin. It looked reddish and milky at the same time, like the yoke from an egg that had gone bad.

She knew the facts. Everyone had abandoned her. No one loved her. Not George. Not Max. Not that puny little embarrassment Elijah. No one. Gretchen was dead and she was next.

But not without a fight. They would pay. They would all pay...

"Felicity? Did you hear me? I said, can I get you anything?"

The crescent of Annie's face hung in front of her. Felicity saw the concerned pitch of her brow and thought how Annie seemed the type of girl who would worry at her own birthday party if everyone was having a good time.

This struck Felicity as funny.

She cracked a smile, then widened it so broadly she was

sure Annie could see her teeth reflected in the moonlight. Felicity cleared her throat. Phlegm squeezed into the pit of her mouth and she spat it out onto the floor. She inhaled the cold air between them and said in a low clear voice: "You heard me, bitch. I said, 'KILL MAX.'"

And to punctuate the sentiment, she laughed.

Annie backed away toward the open door. "I'll see what I can do about that soda."

Felicity heard the door close. Annie's feet scuffled away, across the hallway and down the stairs. Alone, she became aware of the complete and utter silence in the room.

It was totally new to her.

"Really?" Felicity shouted. "Even you???"

She waited. Listened. Unfortunately, it was true.

Even her voices had abandoned her.

"Well, fuck you, too!" she yelled at no one.

Felicity shivered again. Actually she could have used a blanket. Shit, she should have asked for one.

She got on her feet and made her way around the room, hands extended, squinting her eyes even though there was nothing to see. Her fingers found something in the corner, something big and sinister. The wardrobe.

Bingo.

Felicity opened the double doors and blindly rummaged inside.

Something warm was bound to be in there.

CHAPTER SEVENTEEN

Frogs. Locusts. Darkness.

Elijah found his way to the fireplace. Atop the mantle, his fingers traced the outline of an old brass box of matches. He tried to ignite them but the strike-plate proved useless against the soft, slightly-damp matches. With each match's strikeout, he felt the temperature drop. He kept doing it anyway. It was the only thing keeping him sane.

Frogs. Locusts. Darkness. Flies. Boils.

Elijah knew the names of all the Apostles and all of the kings and all of the books in the Bible frontwards and backwards. It was his specialty. Now he couldn't remember something as simple as the Ten Plagues of Egypt.

Frogs. Locusts. Darkness. Flies. Boils. Blood?

Which plagues was he missing? If Annie was right, how many more plagues did the spirits have left to send?

If *Annie was right. But how could she be?*

Spirits, Wiccans, plagues, and flat-out murder—all these thoughts swam inside his head, fighting for dominance, until one outweighed the rest:

Where was God in all this? Where was his *God?*

George limped over and knelt down with a wince. He produced a lighter from his jeans pocket and flicked it several times to the same result as Elijah with his matches.

"None of the lighters are working. Those matches are shit. I guess your Nana didn't believe in buying flashlights."

Elijah frowned. George had a particular skill for making an already bad situation even worse. "She mentioned one time about getting a propane generator. If it's anywhere, it would be in the barn." Elijah turned around. "Max, did you see anything when you were in there?"

Max, his broad figure silhouetted by the red moon outside, stared out the window and said nothing.

Elijah didn't need to see what Max was staring at. He knew.

He felt the temperature in the room drop even lower.

Elijah whispered to George. "Maybe we should bring Gretchen's body inside."

"And get hit by who knows what? Uh-uh. Not me."

George returned his focus to the lighter that wouldn't light. Elijah returned his to the matches that wouldn't ignite.

Frogs. Locusts. Darkness. Flies. Boils. Blood. Lice. Disease.

Two more and he would have it.

"So what are we gonna do?" George's tone implied he expected Elijah to take care of it, as always.

"I suppose I can go check the barn," Elijah hemmed, none too eager to assume the role of leader.

George shook his head impatiently. "No, I meant about... Annie."

Elijah had almost forgotten about her. Almost. "What about her?"

"What if she brought this on us? You know, with her witchcraft?"

"She said she was trying to protect us."

George seemed personally offended. "And you believe her?"

Elijah didn't know *what* to believe anymore. "What happened to believing all of this was nature?"

"That was before I almost got my face chewed off by locusts." George clutched Elijah's shoulder, partly for balance but mostly for emphasis. "I was going to tell you this eventually. But while you were gone... she put a move on me."

Elijah's gut dropped. *"Annie* did?"

"Yeah. Like the moment you were gone, she was all over me. We kissed..."

Annie kissed George?

"... but I broke it off."

George kissed Annie?

"Now, I know I've been a shitty friend…"

That was understating it.

"… but even you know I wouldn't do that on my own. I mean, what do we know about her? Really?"

I knew she wanted to be a nun. That's about it.

George slapped his hand on Elijah's shoulder once more. "I'm telling you… we shouldn't trust her… and don't pretend you're not listening because *I know you're thinking this too.*"

How could he? Elijah stopped thinking a while ago. He'd forgotten how.

Footsteps bounded down the stairs. Annie, appearing to have less trouble seeing in the dark than the rest of them, made a straight line to them.

"Guys," she whispered, urgency in her voice. "Felicity's in bad mental shape."

"Yeah? Well, Max isn't exactly all there himself," Elijah muttered flatly.

She stole a glance to Max—he was still rocking by the window, his eyes locked on the outside.

Even in the dark Elijah could see Annie shudder.

"The sooner we get some light in here, the better," she said, stating the obvious.

George tried his lighter again and got nothing. He threw the useless object into the darkness. "Elijah says there might be a generator in the barn."

Annie brightened. "Good. I'll go."

Elijah, unwilling and unable to spend a second more in the cabin, said, "No, I will."

"I'll go with you," Annie insisted.

They both went toward the direction of the door when Max's low, wounded voice cut through the room. "You don't have a spell to raise the dead, do you, Annie?"

"Sorry, I don't, Max," she answered.

"I didn't think so," he answered back, still not turning around. "You all think if I pray hard enough, like a good little boy, Gretchen will come back?"

Even Elijah, the most faithful, knew it didn't work that way. "Max, we all know you didn't kill Gretchen. It was an accident. We'll defend you."

"You know I ain't leaving here alive." Max chortled, feverishly scratching at his head.

Elijah felt the temperature in the room drop yet again— or maybe it was the blood in his veins turning to ice— when a rattling noise started outside.

And didn't stop.

Annie opened the door.

Elijah recognized it immediately, cursing himself for forgetting.

Hail.

Stones as small as cherries, others as big as oranges, battered the ground. They ricocheted off the overhang covering the porch, sounding as if they might pound through at any minute.

Elijah took a look at the field in front of him; it was completely covered in white balls.

So was Gretchen's body.

Before he could allow the image to sink into his brain, Annie led him by the hand off the porch, down the steps and toward the barn. They were struck about the head and shoulders as they zigged and zagged, slipping in the mud and dodging hail stones the size of softballs. The shiver that ran up and down Elijah's spine seemed to be in complete agreement with Max.

None of us are getting out of here alive.

―――――――――――

They stumbled through the half-open double doors, dusting hail frost and ice chips off their shoulders. Elijah, breathing heavy, waited for his eyes adjust to the dark. Annie scanned the hay bales and rusty tools strewn along the wall. She pointed to a door under the loft. "I guess we can search that back room."

Elijah stared at the ground and leaned on a beam for support.

"Hello? Elijah? Are you okay?"

He hadn't planned to pick an argument with Annie right then, right there, but he felt he had to. Before it was too late.

"What I don't get," he began, "out of everything that's

happened here this evening, is… *you told me you wanted to be a nun!*"

"I did, Elijah," she said, a touch of defensiveness in her voice. "And I told you I wanted to embrace life, not hide from it. *'Do what thou wilt and harm none'* sounded a lot better to me than *'Do what I say or burn forever in Hell.'*"

Elijah turned away. It was easier to be angry if he didn't have to face her directly.

Annie countered by stepping in front of him and lifting his head. With a half-cocked smile and shining the gentlest eyes he'd ever seen, she explained: "I believe God is a choice we make for ourselves. It doesn't mean I stopped believing in a Higher Power, Elijah. I just chose a better god for me, that's all."

"That's what I don't get!" Elijah burst. He took a step away from her, his heart racing, his voice rising higher and higher. "You don't get to choose. When God took my parents in the most horrific way possible, was that a choice? When I was forced to be raised by a holy rolling horror movie-watching grandma who makes me hide my comic books, clip her toenails on Fridays and massage her back on Saturdays… was that a *choice*? YOU DON'T GET TO CHOOSE YOUR GOD! God *is*. God exists. And God is *CRUEL*."

And there it was. The mountain of frustration and panic and pain that was bottled in him for a lifetime erupted and exploded out into the open…

… and flung onto poor Annie.

Her head bowed down to her chest. It didn't rise again for what seemed a very long time.

"Hey, listen," she started, her voice soft to match the stillness in the barn. "It's okay, Elijah. I understand. And I'm sorry if my witchiness came as a surprise. It's not something you tell guys on a first date. But I was going to tell you before we…*if* we were going to do it."

"Like you were going to tell me all about you and George?"

Annie stepped back as if she'd just been sucker punched. "W-w-what?!"

Elijah did not enjoy seeing her squirm. "He told me all about it."

"It was just a kiss. I was hurt. I was confused. Besides, you broke up with me. Remember?"

"And good thing I did. I mean, you're a witch who goes to Catholic school. Can you imagine what people would think? What would my Nana think?"

"Does it *matter* what people think?"

"It does when I can't trust you."

Elijah saw all the fight go out of Annie.

She recovered slowly, clearing her throat. Her eyes narrowed; her tone was ice. "You're right, Elijah. I should have told you all those things sooner. I had a gut feeling about you. About you and me, actually, and what we could discover together. I took a chance. Now I see I was completely wrong about you. For giving me that clarity, I thank you."

With that, she marched toward the small back room of the barn and slammed the door shut.

Elijah was a flurry of emotions. It felt good to speak his mind, to stand up for himself, but it was the satisfaction of squashing a butterfly under a boot. His father had warned him not to be an asshole. And here he was: King Asshole of Devil's Catch.

He picked this fight; now he had to fix it.

He raced after Annie when something heavy and metallic swung from the dark and awarded Elijah with a blow across the face.

CHAPTER EIGHTEEN

Elijah sat up on the barn floor and wiped the blood seeping from his split lip. He found the shovel he'd just mistakenly and stupidly stepped on.

He thought people only did that in cartoons.

With a heavy grunt he heaved it across the barn where it landed at the feet of a large man.

"Havin' yourself quite a night, aren't you, Elijah?"

The man stood over six feet tall, broad-shouldered. His accent was homespun but familiar.

Very familiar.

"Who... who are you?" Elijah stammered, dreading the answer.

The dark giant bent down to pick up the shovel and, rising, tipped his old-fashioned parson's hat. Its brim created a sinister halo around his head. "The name's Reverend Bob Anderson of the Radio Church of God. I believe you have heard some of my work."

The clouds parted momentarily to let in a beam of moonlight from the holes in the roof. The old man's face was bluish and rotting, decomposed and mummy-like. His eyes were dark sockets with small flecks of hay inside them. The only thing bright about him was his teeth, a sinister row of sharpened edges that occasionally twinkled when they caught the light.

"Appears to me like you got quite the problem here." The reverend tossed the shovel onto his shoulder as casually as if he was heading out into the fields. He leaned down conspiratorially to Elijah. Thick, greenish drool hissed from his blue lips. "And the problem goes by the name of Fornication."

Elijah scrambled on his open palms until his back was flush with the wall. "I-I don't know what you're talking about!"

Trapped, he could only watch Reverend Bob lift his head and hands toward the ceiling and deliver a passionate sermon, live and in person.

"The Lord came to me in a vision!" he announced, pausing to glance back down at Elijah. "The Lord said '*get thee to the mountaintop so ye may prepare thyself for the End Times.*' And we did. For ten long years I tended my flock, readying their souls so that they may receive the gift of Heaven. My only contact with the outside world was my nightly broadcast, where I gave ample warning of its impending destruction. Finally the fatal day arrived, the terrible doomsday date of May the First, Nineteen Thirty-Seven! The day came... and then..."

Elijah swore he saw the reverend shrug.

"It went. My flock grew restless. They started to question me..."

The reverend bent to one knee, putrid breath spilling over Elijah's face as it coursed over his razor-like grin. "But I knew it was just a test. For God had come to me a second time to warn me that this ground upon which we are standing is accursed. The Lord said unto me, *'On a full moon you will abstain from all acts of sexual congress, for it is the Devil Himself who wishes to fornicate with you. He will pass through your holy blood and be reborn into a single immaculate body, and through it, he would wreak vengeance upon our kingdoms, lay waste to our temples, until he finally destroys Paradise itself!'*"

Elijah stumbled to his feet only to fall again. He reached out with his hands to push himself to his knees. His palms came back wet with blood that wasn't his. The blood was dark, blackened, cold, sticky. The floor was caked with the stuff.

"But alas... they did not listen..."

Elijah saw them all. The reverend's congregation. They were lying side by side, stacked like cordwood. Their chests were open, their faces pale and ghostly. Rustic clothes—black pants and stiff white shirts—adorned the bodies. Felt hats covered in blood and gore lay scattered on the hay.

"I began first with the men. Then the women. Then the children... then myself..."

More bodies appeared before the barn doors, piled on top of each other, as if caught in mid-escape. Only when the moonlight hit them could Elijah see that they were children, their eyes lifeless and directed at the sky, their tiny hands clutching gaping wounds.

Elijah scrambled to his feet. When he spun around, the man's ravaged, rotting, blistered face was next to his.

"It was the only way to save our souls from the demon Fornication. Yet you and your friends choose to desecrate our holy sacrifice. So I prayed for God to send you warnings in the form of the Ten Plagues of Egypt..."

The reverend paused. Elijah detected a sigh in his voice.

"But alas," he continued, "your dumb hormones got you confused... they got you running around like a pack of wild animals so hungry for sex you're killing each other!"

Elijah wedged himself into the corner. His fingers found a dusty tarp. Elijah threw it off, desperately hoping for an escape route.

He found the generator.

Elijah fumbled through dust and cobwebs to get it working. If this was another one of his weird dreams, perhaps light would make it go away.

The reverend lifted an accusing finger at Elijah as he approached. "And you... you would make a witch the

Devil's Concubine... a witch with her false thoughts and practices. Touch not the impure thing, Elijah, or else Satan will rise from Hell and beget a son of mortal woman. I sent you a vision of what would be if you continue on your path. Do you not remember?"

Elijah's skin squirmed with the memory of flames licking his face, Annie's screams from her half-naked body, both of them perishing in their own circle of Dante's Inferno.

"W-w-what do you want with me?" he stammered.

Reverend Bob held the shovel above his head—only now, the shovel was an axe. "Your salvation, boy. Before the lust in you brings about the beast. How many more plagues must be sent before you are washed in the blood of the lamb...?"

Elijah's hand found the generator switch.

Reverend Bob shouted, "Remember, we're fighting the Devil Himself! Fight Him, Elijah! Fight like your good Nana says. And always remember, son... GOD HAS HIS FINGER ON YOUR HEART!"

Elijah shut his eyes, flipped the generator's switch to the ON position and braced himself for the axe blade.

Instantly, the barn lights flashed to life.

Elijah opened one eye. Then the other.

There was no blood caked on the walls. No innards spilled between the hay bales. No bodies sliced open like in some horror movie. No evidence of the reverend remained.

Just his old fashioned parson's hat.

Elijah, his sanity having left him a long time ago, reached out to where the hat lay on the floor when the good reverend, now transparent and ghostly, grabbed it from him. The apparition dusted the hat over his arm before placing it on his head.

"It don't worry me none if you won't listen, boy. You'll finish *yourselves* off before the evening's done." He gave a wink from his empty eye socket and he promptly vanished.

A hand touched Elijah's shoulder.

Elijah leapt straight up; he twisted himself around mid-air to see who or what it was behind him.

It was only Annie. The rest of the barn stood empty.

"Oh great," she said, as if the floor hadn't just been littered with hundreds of corpses. "You found the generator."

She waved her hand, beckoning him toward the back room.

"I found something too…"

CHAPTER NINETEEN

The cabin's front window was fogged over with condensation from the sudden hailstorm. Max smeared it clear with his hand. Icy stones of all sizes, shapes and degrees filled the porch and front yard. All he saw was Gretchen. Lifeless and faceless, her right leg bent at an awkward angle, her tiny arms stretched over her head. He couldn't remove himself from mourning over the body of his girlfriend — wait, *ex*-girlfriend. Shit, was she technically a girlfriend if he had killed her?

The clouds shifted. Moonlight glinted on Gretchen's lidless eyes. Then, as if suddenly self-aware, her head swiveled toward him.

Her jaw creaked open.

Max, terrified, ducked away.

He was seeing things, he convinced himself. He rubbed his eyes and slowly, hesitatingly, peeked his head back to the window.

Her head was facing him, her mouth wide open as if she were giving the world's biggest yawn. Her head *had* moved, yes, but it was gravity shit. Gretchen herself didn't move. She couldn't anymore.

Except her leg was bent on the left side this time.

Max tried to remember how she lay mere seconds ago. Nothing came to him, nothing but the same steady whoosh of confusion and shame pounding through his head, coupled with a persistent ringing in his ears that only seemed to get louder...

A loud thump clattered above his head. Black, rotted wood showered his head.

George had just thrown a log at the wall.

Max spun around. "The hell?" he asked.

"Didn't you hear me?" George said, still fiddling with the matches. "I said hand me that lighter. I think I almost got something here."

Under his doo rag, Max's head still itched something fierce.

"You all right?" George asked.

"You know, I think Annie's right about the house playing with our heads," he answered, scratching his head for the umpteenth time. "I can feel it sending me bad thoughts, like they were... like they were digging into my brain."

Scratching through the fabric just wasn't getting the job done. Max reached up and took off the bandana. He immediately felt better.

"Where's that lighter?"

"On the table."

His shin found the table first, and after some blind groping, Max located the lighter. He wound his way to the fireplace where George finally got one of the old fashioned matches to light. Max brought the lighter next to the flame and flicked it. Whatever remaining fluid was left fizzled to life with a green, noxious flame, bathing George's triumphant face in an eerie glow. Max stared at the long, dancing flame with relief. Something as simple as making a fire made it seem like everything was going to be all right.

But there was something he had to address first.

"You know, George, um," he stammered, "what happened between me and Felicity... in the barn... you know... it wasn't personal."

George turned to him, a dead serious look on his face made more serious by the stark green flame he held. "You tried to fuck her. Why would I think it personal?"

A tiny grin crept across George's lips, followed by a full smile.

Max, again relieved, smiled in return. He still had his friend.

The power surged and all the lights came back on.

Max flicked off the lighter. "Figures."

When Max saw his friend's face again, he saw George's

eyes were bugging out. "What? George, was is it? What's wrong with you?"

George backed away cautiously, hands out, as if he was staring down a giant grizzly bear. "Max... your *head*...!"

"Huh? What is it? What's the matter?"

"Don't... don't touch it..."

Max's head itched. "Don't touch *what*? What is it? What's wrong?"

Max touched his head with one finger and felt something wet and bumpy... and living. Whatever it was, it was stuck to his head.

Or was it... *in* his head?

"Max, remember," George shouted, halfway across the room. "The important thing is not to pan—"

Too late.

Max bolted into the kitchen and searched for anything that could give a reflection. He rifled through drawers, finding only rusty silverware. There was no microwave, not in this ancient junk heap, and all the frying pans were cast iron and black. But there! Finally! A toaster. He grabbed it and raised it up to his face.

"Max, no!" George shouted, hobbling into the kitchen. "Don't do it! Don't look!! Wait!!!"

Max ignored him, angling the greasy toaster so he could see the back of his head.

Something white and long, fat and plump like a hot dog, crawled in and out of a hole on the side of his skull.

Max wiped the grease off the toaster with his sleeve in case he was seeing things. He held it back up again.

Now there were *two* of the creeping white sausages, inching and wriggling in and out of his head.

Max held the toaster to his other side. He saw his head was a nest of holes, resembling a slice of Swiss cheese. A dozen or so white worms burrowed inside them, squiggling on top of each other to get at the meat inside.

It wasn't ringing in his ears that he had been hearing—

It was *munching*.

Max recalled an old song his teacher used to sing in grade school around Halloween: *The worms crawl in, the worms crawl out...*" He retched a dry heave before dropping the toaster to the floor and seizing the kitchen counter for support.

George was a few feet away, hand cupped over his mouth.

Max pleaded in a tinny voice. "Help me... George?... Please... get 'em off of me..."

But George backed away, hands up not to reach out to Max but to defend against him.

"George, help me," Max whimpered, stumbling after him. His head ached—no, it *throbbed*. And the worms, the maggots were slinking all over his forehead, blurring his vision, tickling his ear.

"George... HELP ME!"

George's back slammed against the kitchen wall,

nowhere to go. Max lurched at him, the giant crawling white slugs dropping onto his shoulders and falling to his feet. The maggots and worms fell to the floor and burst open, their innard gut juice splattering on the linoleum like liquid from a water balloon.

"George, you brought me here. Now you gotta help me—*arrgghhh!!!*"

Max doubled over. The pain in his head was too intense. He was going mad, the parasites chewing away his last ounce of his sanity. He heard the sound of the maggots' feasting building, building, building—

Until he heard a *pop* and saw nothing more.

———————

George wiped away the chunks of brain and dead maggots from his face in time to see Max's lifeless body slump to the floor, his shoulders coming to rest against an ancient stove the color of olives.

His head looked like a jack-o'-lantern that had been kicked in.

George slowly backed away from the bloody carcass in the kitchen when he saw Felicity clomp down the stairs. Her hair was mess, frazzled and sticking in the air like she had put her finger in a socket. She carried a shotgun at her side, so big and old it took both hands to hoist it.

Both barrels were smoking.

"The hell did you get t-t-*that*?" George stammered.

Felicity aimed the shotgun at him and sobbed her reply: "Your turn."

George ducked as the gun discharged with a thunderous explosion. The wall above his head splintered into drywall and shotgun pellets and God knows how many dried-out, desiccated rat carcasses. He bolted for the door.

Felicity called out, "Red light!"

The doorjamb exploded above his head.

George stopped.

Felicity racked the double barrels down, popping out two smoking shells, and refilled them from a seemingly endless supply in her pocket. She descended the stairs, step by step, her voice dry and cracked and shaking.

"You were so nice to me in the beginning. So I thought, sure, I'll spend the weekend with you, throw you a little bang, spread a little cheer." Felicity broke into tears. "Did I have to go to HELL for it???"

George surveyed his options. There was too much room to leap for the door without getting a spine full of buckshot and there was nowhere to hide if he somehow made it back into the kitchen. This was it. All his plots and schemes, every Sunday mass he sat through and every class he attended, had led to this: hands in the air, helpless to move, staring in the face of the girl he had wanted so badly, so desperately to bang, as she readied to end his life.

The only thing left for him to do was what he did best... smirk.

George said, "And here I thought the fact you were crazy made you hot."

"Crazy?" Felicity shouted, her voice growing more frenzied. "CRAZY? YOU FUCKING IDIOT... I HAVE A DISEASE!"

"Which one is it again? Bipolar, manic depression or did your parents not give you enough attention?"

Felicity tilted her head. "Is there medication for that last one?"

The air grew still; he had run out of comebacks.

She raised the shotgun to his head. "Take this as our official breakup notice," she garbled, her finger pushing on the trigger. "Night-night George..."

The front door sprang open.

There, in the doorway, stood Gretchen. Bow in hand, arrow rightly quivered, her bloody arm bent as she pulled back, back, back. George couldn't look away from her skinless face, the hinges of her jaw, her exposed teeth, her golf-ball eyeballs staring straight at Felicity.

Gretchen fired.

The first arrow snagged Felicity in the shoulder. She dropped the shotgun. It fired harmlessly into the wall.

Gretchen released another arrow, then another. The second arrow nailed Felicity's left hand to the stairwell wall. The third pinned her right wrist to the other side.

As Gretchen slid one more arrow into the bow, Felicity, hanging crucified above the stairs, looked down at her—what was left of her—and in a desperate, shaking shrill voice, screamed her final insult: "FUCK YOU, BITCH!"

Gretchen let go the final arrow. With pinpoint accuracy, it flew into Felicity's mouth and pinned her head to the wall, killing her instantly.

Drool slid down Gretchen's fleshless chin. She dropped her bow. With her spittle-covered teeth spread wide, Gretchen gurgled something that sounded like, "*Hhuuuckkk kyuu tuu, glitch.*"

Gretchen moved toward George, that same skull smile fixed on her gleaming, bloody head. He cowered as she slid past him to find Max, with his caved-in head, sprawled on the kitchen floor.

Through the kitchen door, George saw Gretchen kneel beside his body. Her raspy, ragged voice wheezed from her fleshless lips, "*Vheeeedeeeee gaaaaarrrdd.*" Then she too expired, falling onto Max like two logs stacked on a fire.

George was alone. The only lungs still breathing and the only heart beating in the room were his. He closed his eyes, thanking his lucky stars... no, giving thanks to God for sparing him when...

Snap, fizz, crack.

The radio's remains limped back to life. Broken tubes sparked. The dangling dial glowed. Ozone wafted from the sizzling metallic guts. From the splintered pile in the corner, Reverend Bob's voice beckoned from the shattered speaker and echoed in the blood-splattered room:

"And once more Moses stretched forth his rod toward heaven: and the Lord sent thunder and hail, and the fire ran along upon the ground..."

George should have raced from the cabin, or reached for an axe to chop the remains of the radio into coffee grounds.

Instead, he slumped to the floor, grateful to be living, and raptly listened to the words from the radio. For the first time ever, he found them comforting.

CHAPTER TWENTY

Elijah expected to see rusted farm tools in the back room or cobwebbed tractor tires lying in storage. Anything except what he now saw.

It was a vintage radio station, packed to the rafters with transmitters, receivers, meters, amplifiers, microphones, ear phones. They all looked antique to Elijah's modern eyes, but assuming this had been amassed in the 1930s, it was state of the art.

Annie picked up a decaying earpiece. "This must be where they recorded the sermons we've been hearing. And look..."

She opened a crate that contained old phonograph records. She reached in and handed him one.

The yellowed album cover read: *The Radio Church of God Reads Passages From the Bible, Featuring...The Reverend Bob Anderson.* A black and white photo showed a smiling congregation posed in front of a familiar barn.

This barn. Nana's barn.

The sea of all white, all smiling faces looked barber fresh, the men with slicked-back hair and handlebar moustaches, the women in tight curls and little, if any, makeup. Standing in the center of the congregation was none other than Reverend Bob himself. He stood an inch or two taller than his flock, a thick Bible in his sausage fingers. His robe was black, his collar white. His hair was as slick as his smile.

And his eyes... he actually *had* eyes.

Elijah shivered, recalling the rotted sockets he had seen only minutes earlier.

The group proudly held a sign across them—a mattress sheet—upon which they had crudely scrawled "GOODBYE EARTH!"

Annie's voice was small, almost reverent. "They were a doomsday cult. This barn was their church, Elijah. I wonder what happened to them."

Elijah turned to her, eyes flat and dull to match his affectless voice. "The reverend killed his followers. Men, women, children. All because he believed they'd sire the devil if they had sex. Then he killed himself."

Annie arched one eyebrow. "You *knew* all this?"

Elijah knew if anyone would believe what he was about to say, it would be Annie. "He told me. Just now. He spoke to me. He kinda looked like the Quaker Oats guy. He tried to chop me with an axe. He even mentioned you..."

Her other eyebrow went up.

Elijah continued. "He also said I would make you the devil's concubine if I had sex with you."

Annie edged her way back into the barn. "Okay, great, well... good to know... uh... I'd better check on the others."

With each step she quickened her pace. Elijah ran after her. He grabbed her arm just before she reached the entrance. She stood with her back to him, her shoulders quivering. Elijah whipped her around to face him. "You believe me, don't you Annie?"

Fresh tears glinted in her eyes. "Look, Elijah, just because I believe in the Goddess doesn't mean I believe in Casper the Friendly Ghost."

"What? Who said anything about—"

Her face hardened. "You don't have to make up stories to give me reasons you don't want to sleep with me. I got the message loud and clear. *Multiple* times."

Elijah pleaded. "No Annie, please, that's not true."

"Sure it isn't," she sarcastically huffed as she slid open the double doors to reveal George, shotgun in hand.

Time slowed to a crawl as Elijah witnessed the twin barrels explode in a flash of light and smoke. The bullets struck Annie and threw her back nearly eight feet. She landed against a hay bale and crumpled to the floor.

"Annie!"

Elijah rushed to her and lifted her head up, expecting

half of her face to be gone. Her hair slid off of a ragged wound on her left shoulder. It looked ugly, but not fatal. Blood seeped through her teeth from where she had bitten the inside of her lip.

"Ouch," she chuckled joylessly.

Elijah turned on George, tears in his eyes. "*Why,* George? *Why* would you do that?"

George said nothing as he racked down the barrels and shoved several fresh shells into the gun. He limped forward, pointing the gun at Annie once more. "If she hadn't have come here, everyone else would still be alive."

Elijah felt the hairs on the back of his neck stand on end. "What do you mean... *everyone else*?"

"I just saw Max's head get blown apart. I just saw Felicity swallow an arrow fired at her by a recently come-back-to-life-and-then-die-again Gretchen. THIS KIND OF STUFF IS NOT SUPPOSED TO HAPPEN AT A SEX PARTY!"

"But... how is this *Annie's* fault?"

George advanced. "Why do you think she's here, Elijah? Think for a minute. Why did she agree to spend a weekend with you? Because she *likes* you? No one likes you... *I* don't even like you..."

"Come on, George, you know that's not true..."

"Do you think it's easy being handsome and hanging around the likes of *you*? I'm meant to be *cool*! And I was going to be after this weekend until you invited Sabrina the Teenage Witch over here with her demon ways and sorcery."

Annie sat up and wiped the blood off her chin with the back of her good arm, visibly offended. "Demon ways? Sorcery? What are you talking about!"

"You tried to seduce me!"

"*Seduce* you? You dope, I was *talking* with you."

Elijah saw the slightest shimmer of doubt pass across George's face as the shotgun slightly lowered. "But you… you kissed me."

"Yeah. Then I threw up right after. Remember *that* part?"

George shook his head and raised the rifle once more.

Elijah positioned his body in front of Annie.

"Get out of the way, Elijah."

Elijah did just the opposite. He dug in his feet and pressed his chest against the barrels of the gun. "George, listen to me. This is not you. I can explain what's going on here if you'll give me the chance. But if you're going to shoot Annie, you're gonna have to shoot me fir—"

Click. Click.

The gun jammed.

Elijah looked down at the gun which should have been splattered with his own guts, then up at the friend who attempted to kill him. Looking into his crazed eyes, all Elijah could do was cry out, "You… DICK!"

Elijah charged George and grabbed the gun, but George

was stronger and yanked it free of his hands. This time the gun went off. The rotted wall just above Annie's head exploded with the first blast.

George aimed again at Annie. Elijah launched himself at George, knocking them both to the ground. The gun discharged again, blasting a gaping hole through the barn roof high above. Dust and splinters and kindling and cobwebs rained down upon them.

Elijah lay on the ground, catching his breath, when he saw one of the main support beams, nearly sheared in half by the shotgun blast, give way. He rolled between two hay bales just in time to see roof cave in all around them.

After the dust cleared, Elijah searched for Annie amid the debris.

She was nowhere to be found.

Annie heard the crash behind her as she crawled sideways, favoring her bloody shoulder, into the radio room. She pulled herself up into the old wicker chair in front of the consoles. Sore everywhere, head pounding, she stared at the old-fashioned dials and cords and microphone in front of her. Flying on instinct, Annie found a large switch on the radio transmitter and flicked it up.

The ancient radio hummed to life. The room lit up with the glowing dials. Annie reached for the microphone and heard a telltale squawk as she moved it closer to her face.

"Hello," she cried breathlessly. "Hello? Can anyone hear me? I need help..."

Distant crackles greeted her impassioned plea as she tried again and again, "Help, someone, please help us!"

Annie noted a second hole for the microphone cord. She unplugged it and tried the other input jack, picturing herself as one of those old-time phone operators. The microphone squawked again.

"Hello?" she cried listlessly, assuming her voice was just drifting into the ether. "Hello, emergency, emergency, we need—"

Without fanfare, an almost bored voice interrupted, "Ranger Headquarters. We're reading you. What's your emergency?"

Annie was baffled and relieved by the question. Her emergency? What the hell *was* her emergency? That plagues were coming back into vogue? That her friends were chopping off each other's faces with shovels and blowing each other to smithereens with shotguns?

She tried the less-is-more approach. "I need help. I'm up at the cabin at Devil's Catch. I'm wounded. Two—no, three people are dead..."

A large shape passed by the window just to her left. It could have been Elijah racing toward the cabin. No, she thought, too big. George, maybe?

The dispatcher's voice cut in. "Where is this cabin, exactly?"

The shape passed again. Annie ignored the dispatcher and approached the window. She tugged her sleeve over her wrist and wiped off decades of grime. All she saw was the wind swaying the trees outside.

Again, the dispatcher asked, "Hello, miss? We need your location. Where is Devil's Catch, exactly?"

Annie wiped away more grime and leaned in closer.

Her jaw dropped.

The shape wasn't in front of her. She was looking at a reflection of what was *behind* her.

Annie spun around, dropping the heavy microphone onto the hardwood floor. Reverend Bob stood in the open doorway, eyeless, axe in hand, a giant shadow with an evil grin. She backed away as far as she could, but the room was small. Reverend Bob lurched forward, eyeless, heavy feet stomping on the hollow floor, when Annie remembered the words she said to the group.

"Y-y-you're a spirit. Spirits can't hurt me."

The reverend's spirit smiled for a fraction of a second, then he lunged, the axe off his shoulder and airborne. Annie barely had time to leap out of the way before the blade slammed into the work table and split it in two. Radio equipment crashed to the floor, snapping and sizzling and sputtering out. Decades of dust fumed around the wreckage.

The weapon next smashed through a cabinet and into a wall, sending chunks of wood and mold everywhere.

Annie bounced around the room, her eyes fixated on the shiny axe blade.

The reverend lashed out with the blade once more. Instead of pivoting, Annie tripped over her own feet and tumbled so hard on the floor her teeth clattered together. Reverend Bob sneered as she turned onto her backside and scuttled away on all fours. His smile was vicious, lips flecked with spit, as he slammed the axe into the floor repeatedly, surrounding her with vicious gashes, the wood planks coughing up splinters by the dozens.

Annie backed into the wall. She watched him stand above her, triumphant, the axe hovering high above his head.

His velvet smooth voice was calm but forceful. "Do not turn to mediums or spiritists—"

Annie cut him off and chanted. "*Luna, Luna, Luna, Diana, Luna, Luna, Luna, Diana, bless me, bless me, bless me, Luna, Luna, Luna...*"

This angered the reverend. He raised his voice and his axe even higher, poised to strike. "Do not seek them out to be defiled by them!"

Annie met his raised voice with hers. "*Guardian spirit, take wing upon the thousand winds and carry my will—*"

Raising his voice even louder, Reverend Bob roared in direct competition. "FOR I AM THE LORD THY GOD—"

Annie thundered her voice to match his. "*STAND OVER AND PROTECT ME—*"

"DO NOT ALLOW—"

"WITH MY WILL—"

"A SORCERESS—"

"I WISH IT SO!"

"TO LIVE!!"

"BE OFF!!!"

The axe descended with a vengeance, blade glinting in the backlight.

Annie shut her eyes.

No-no-no-no-nooooo.

On the fifth no, her skull still intact, she opened her eyes.

The room was empty. Reverend Bob was gone.

She could breathe now.

Annie rose, feeling very pleased with herself. "Wow, I'm getting really good at this magic stuuuuuuuufffff—"

The floor gave way beneath her, heaving with a giant *crrrrrack*. Annie and a thousand splinters collapsed into the damp, grimy basement.

She landed on her side. The floor was cold and damp. A shaft of light beamed through the Annie-sized hole in the floor above and illuminated a gruesome tableau.

She was surrounded by skeletons. Dozens of them. Most were mummified. The rest were skeletons, cracked skulls leaning on bony necks. Cobwebs covered their gaping eye holes and wove their skeletal jaws together. They were dressed much as they had been in the picture upstairs—severe black pants and white shirts for the men, dowdy lace dressed for the women. In the bony fingers of a few sagged open hymnals, pages yellowed and leather covers cracked.

Staring, open-mouthed, Annie finally found the breath—and the nerve—to scream.

She ran to escape but smacked face-first into another skeleton, this time a familiar one: the corpse of Reverend Bob, black coat and white collar, parson's hat and all. His jaw cracked off at her impact and fell onto her shoulder. The rest of him crumbled to dust.

Annie squealed. She wiped away the decomposed jaw bone of Reverend Bob when her back hit something hard and wooden. A ladder. She reached for it, sobbing without tears. She pulled her body upward, anxiously, quickly, contrite from the knowledge that while spirits couldn't kill you, they *could* hurt you...

And right now every bone in Annie's body hurt like a motherfucker.

———————

Elijah stumbled over the splintered beams and shingle piles strewn about the barn. Off kilter, his balance shaken, he shook his blurred vision into focus.

His foot tapped the shotgun.

Elijah bent down to reach it when George leaped on his back. He grabbed Elijah's hair by the fistful and pummeled his face.

But as big as George was, the fire had gone out of him. On a regular day, George could have knocked Elijah into next week. Now his punches felt more like mosquito stings.

"George!" Elijah shouted, slapping his friend's hands away. "Listen to me... let me *explain*! This place was a church. It belonged to a cult leader who believed sex is evil. *He's* the one behind it. Not Annie."

George paused his half-hearted beating, eyes growing heavy lidded with exhaustion and skepticism. He looked around at the shattered roof, the leaning walls, the bloody hay bales.

"This shithole was a *church*?"

"Yes." Elijah saw his chance and bucked George off of him.

"A church against sex?"

"Yes!"

"And the plagues happened because they didn't want us to have sex in their place?"

Elijah suddenly knew what a broken record sounded like. "YES!"

George shook his head. "That's the craziest thing I've ever heard."

With a grunt, he charged into Elijah. Elijah's feet flew into the air and he landed hard on his back. His spine felt like it was on fire. He rolled over to stop the pain.

Groaning, arms trembling, he lifted himself up until he felt the gun's steel barrels, pressed between his shoulder blades, pin him back to the earth.

His friend's voice was bitter and cold. "You know what really hurts about all this, Elijah?"

Elijah tried to rise again. With the front of the gun, George shoved him back down.

"It's that you would take her word over mine."

Elijah's fingers dug into the hay-covered floor as George momentarily allowed him to crawl away. George followed him, limping, shotgun raised.

"But you know what? I forgive you…"

Elijah collapsed onto his back. He felt like he was going to faint, but the gun pressed against his forehead brought him back.

George's smile was wicked. His finger crooked around the trigger. "After all, you didn't know she was a witch."

CLANG!

A shovel clocked George on the side of the head. He landed next to Elijah, limp.

Standing in his place was Annie. She looked down at George, shovel at her side. "That's Wiccan, you fucker."

Elijah saw the trap door lying open near the corner of the barn. He smiled up at Annie, half-dazed, sounding like the biggest idiot in the world. "Wow… I never knew the barn had a basement."

Annie smiled in return, as to say *It's okay you're an idiot.*

She extended a hand. Elijah took it. He was mostly dead weight, he knew, but he couldn't help it. Nearly being shot half a dozen times in one night would do that to a guy.

Suddenly George was on his feet and tackled Annie. His shoulder bent her in half at the waist as he carried her halfway across the barn until her head smacked a wooden post with a sickening *pluh-thunk*. She fell at odd angles, pretzel-style, like someone had yanked out her bones.

"ANNIE!" Elijah cried.

Her body did not respond.

George grabbed the shotgun and sprinted toward Elijah. Like an old movie cowboy charging some Indians, George cocked the gun running and aimed it straight at Elijah when his foot caught the blade of a shovel. The handle whizzed through the air and smacked George against the nose, flattening it.

Elijah cringed. He knew that had to have hurt *bad*.

George dropped the gun, hands clasped around the bleeding fountain that was his nose.

Elijah rushed for the gun. As soon as he felt his hands clasp the handle, the barn boomed with laughter.

George's laughter.

"What are you gonna do? Shoot me?" he cackled, blood spouting from his face. "You're too afraid to use that thing. You're too afraid of *everything*. That's why you always do what your Nana says. That's why you're a good little Christian. You're too scared to do anything on your own.

You're just one big fat fraidy cat..."

Elijah placed the recoil pad on his shoulder and locked George in the shotgun's sight. His voice was never deeper when he snarled, "I ain't so afraid."

George, his eyes reflecting fear for once, staggered backwards to run away.

Elijah lowered the gun, winded but triumphant, in time to see George trip over his feet, launch himself through the open trap door and tumble to the basement below. Elijah heard a muffled crunching noise, followed by a groan. He ran to the trap door to look down.

Ten feet below, George had impaled himself on two erect skeletal hands clasped together in prayer. His hands grappled with guts and intestines—*his* guts and intestines—slithering and falling out of his body. Even in his dying state, he gazed up at Elijah, blood trickling from his lips, and managed one of his trademark smirks.

"Next time we bring our own radio, whaddya think?" George said before he closed his eyes and died.

Elijah slammed the trap door shut over his former friend and slid the bolt in place for good.

He ran to Annie. She was moaning into the soft hay that covered the barn floor.

"Annie," he said, gently propping her up against the same pole that had knocked her out.

Her eyes fluttered open and closed, like headlights on a car being jumpstarted.

He grabbed a shoulder, shaking her gently. "Annie, listen to me. You are not allowed to die. You hear me?" Elijah shook her again and waited for Annie to nod.

She did, eyes closed, and weakly muttered, "Why not?"

"Why not? Because... because *my* God won't allow it. You see, all I was wanted to do was find a good girl and do the right thing. But the minute I found a nice girl, a girl I really, really like, I'm swallowing up frog guts and spitting out locust wings. I thought it was God punishing me. But no, He wasn't *my* God... my God's cool. He likes comic books and video games. Sure, He took my parents away, and He let my friends destroy themselves, but He brought me *you*... and you're not going to die because I don't want to believe in a god so cruel... Because God is a choice... like you said... just like love... just like *this*..."

Elijah leaned in and kissed Annie with everything he had.

Her lips did not kiss back.

When he pulled back, her eyes were still closed. Elijah shook her, panicking. "Annie? Annie!"

Annie's eyes opened to half-mast then widened. "Wait a min, are you saying... you *like* me?"

Elijah laughed, thrilled she was still with him. "Yes! I always liked you. I was just..."

"An asshole?"

Annie was back.

"Yeah, okay, sure... I was an asshole. I'm sorry about

that. And I'm sorry my best friend tried to kill you."

Annie chuckled. "Well, you Catholics *do* have a habit of killing witches."

He helped her stand. She got halfway across the barn before she started gagging and coughing and slumping back to the ground. He let her rest for a moment.

Between coughs, she sputtered, "I saw him... The Quaker Oats guy you were talking about... You were right. I'm sorry I didn't believe you."

"It's okay..."

Her cough subsided and she looked at him, real fear in her eyes. "No, it's not. He isn't just going to let us go. His spirit here is strong. Like *mega*-strong... I can feel him watching us right now..."

Elijah sighed. Annie was right. The reverend wasn't going to let them waltz away. Not without a fight.

And suddenly he remembered. "Death of the first born."

"What's that?" she asked, confused.

"Death of the first born," Elijah repeated. "That's the last plague I forgot about."

"Oh," Annie nodded, before adding, "I'm the first born of my siblings."

"I'm an only child."

"Sucks to be us then."

Elijah looked around the remains of the old barn and, determination in his eyes, shouted to the absent reverend.

"Hey old man, listen up! Plague or no plagues, I'm going to get this girl out of here. And when I do, *I'm going to be the best boyfriend she ever had*!!"

"Why wait?"

Annie's voice turned him around. "Huh?"

She gave him a look, one he'd never seen before in his short life. Her pupils were dark, her eyes smoldering... inviting. He locked his eyes onto hers and felt the familiar strange stirring below, the same beehive-in-the-shorts-on-a-hot-day urge the nuns at school said to avoid touching at all costs.

With that one look, Elijah realized he would never care about nuns again.

"Are you saying... since we're both first-borns and we're both going to die anyway...?"

A mischievous grin oozed across Annie's face.

Elijah kissed her once more. This time she kissed back. Warm, lovingly, hungrily. When he pulled back, he rose to his feet and scooped Annie in his arms and proclaimed:

"Let's give the old man a thrill!"

CHAPTER TWENTY-ONE

Elijah kicked the cabin door open and carried Annie across the threshold.

He strode straight past the bodies of Max and Gretchen as they lay clustered in a pool of blood on the kitchen floor.

He strode up the stairs past Felicity, her arms pinned to the wall, her mouth held open by a single fatal arrow.

With each step, he felt stronger.

Inside the master bedroom Elijah lay Annie down on the bed in one swift motion. As she stretched out on the covers, he lit the bedside candle with a nearby match. The glowing light revealed Annie in mid-motion as she removed her bloody sweater and then her lacey black bra. Her breasts stood pert on her pale, lithe body.

Elijah stood there a while, staring, mouth agape.

"What?" Annie laughed, half out of nervousness.

"Pinch me," he said, a trace of uncertainty in his excited

voice.

Annie grinned mischievously. "Ooh, kinky."

She leaned forward on the bed, grinning wide, and gently bit his left nipple through his shirt.

A jolt of electricity sprang from his toes all the way up his zipper.

Definitely *not* a vision.

Elijah took off his shirt and dropped it to the floor. He awkwardly began to unbuckle his belt. Wriggling a finger coyly at him, Annie beckoned him to bed.

"Come here," she croaked, voice husky and thick with desire. She reached for his hands, dragging him down on top of her.

They kissed, softly at first then not softly at all. Elijah propped himself on his elbows to tease off her shirt, adding it to the growing pile of clothes at the foot of the bed. He slid back on top of her as she whispered, "Take off your pants, silly."

Elijah squirmed out of them as their final layers of clothes slid away. She helped the shy virgin into position and, with a single natural push, he melted into her, closing his eyes then opening them again quickly to savor every moment of this.

Oh God… this is great!

Elijah ground harder.

Annie shrieked, sharply, scaring him.

"Are you all right?"

She cast him one of her lazy smiles. "It's the shoulder with the bullet in it. Try not to lean on it."

"Right. Got it."

The bed rocked, the headboard clattered. It bumped against the nightstand.

Oh, God, oh God…

Nana's old perfume bottle wobbled, rolled to the floor and broke.

Oh no…

The smell was instant and far from subtle, but neither were Annie's groans as she drew closer and closer to a climax. Elijah watched the bedside candle, flickering healthily, inch closer and closer to the edge of the nightstand with each passionate thrust of their lovemaking, until finally it fell to the floor.

Oh shit!

There was a familiar *whoosh* sound but it was hard to hear over Annie's squeals as she writhed beneath him. Flames licked the edges of the mattress. As the heat tickled his forearms and sweat began to pool in the small of his back, he spilled the last of himself inside her. Elijah collapsed onto her as the fire raged faster, higher, hotter. Every breath filled his lungs with the heat from the encroaching inferno. Gasping for air, he turned away—

Reverend Bob was standing in the corner, his hands clasped before him. He was shaking his head in both disapproval and pity. "Can't say I didn't warn you."

Elijah hissed at him. "Leave us. NOW."

The reverend took visible offense. "My sympathies to you both," he said sharply, before he turned on his heel, faced the wall and, stepping forward, disappeared into it.

"Elijah," Annie moaned, eyes at half-mast, throat slick with sweat. Her eyes blinked open as she returned to awareness and they grew, wider and wider, as the fire consumed the room. It was above them now, beside them, the curtains alight over the open window. The doorway was a cauldron of fire, with no way in or out.

Elijah saw it all reflected in the dark of Annie's frightened eyes.

Suddenly, a great rumbling sounded in the distance.

"What's that sound?" Annie asked, startling him as she sat up. They heard it together—an advancing, rushing sound growing in intensity somewhere outside the cabin.

"Hold me," was all Elijah could say.

She held him tight and wrapped her limbs around him, and his around hers, bodies naked and sticky with sweat. The roar from outside was deafening. Elijah flinched as little shards of flame broke off from the ceiling and burned holes in the bed sheets. The floor shook. The window rattled. It sounded like a jumbo jet was heading straight toward them.

But it wasn't an airplane Elijah heard.

It sounded more like… splashing.

A giant wave hit the cabin. Water funneled through the

doorway and crashed through the windows. Steam rose.

So did Annie and Elijah.

The bed rose in the awesome rush of water until it pressed against the ceiling with nowhere else to go. Beams cracked and hissed, black from the sudden extremes, hot to cold, dry to wet. The bed broke through the ceiling. All he could see was water, water, water, as the great wave washed away the cabin and barn, washed away the woods, washed away all the dead bodies and skeletons and skulls.

Elijah coughed and sputtered, arms clung around Annie, defending her as she choked and spat. The rushing water carried them away until all he saw were stars and foam and water and Annie and then…

Nothing but light.

4
THE CATCH

Elijah snapped to awareness and blinked his eyes against the brightest light he'd ever seen.

Heaven.

The sky was crystal blue, the clouds puffy and white, the breeze gentle on his face.

Heaven. This was it. I made it —

The squawk of a bullhorn broke his concentration.

He sat up. He focused on a riverbank where a police officer stood, bullhorn in hand.

The officer wasn't alone. Behind him, several squad cars were parked at precarious angles, lights flashing, uniformed officers standing in front of them.

Heaven has cops? Elijah wondered.

The officer on the shore looked mad. Excessive violence mad. He raised the bullhorn to his lips and this time the squawk was followed by stern words. "You there. In the bed. Swim to shore."

Elijah raised his hands above his head in the universal language for *WTF*? He looked down and realized why the officer might have been kind of tiffed.

Elijah was floating on the mattress, in the middle of the lake, naked as a jaybird. Annie, too. She was crawled up in a fetal position next to him, snoring away. They were both shriveled and pale, as if they'd been there for some time. He yanked what remained of the sheets above them and stared back at the shore.

Almost as if waiting for him to come to this realization, the squawk of the bullhorn sounded again as the cop added, "The girl, too."

Elijah nudged Annie awake. She sat up with a snort and, taking her time, her eyes widened as she realized what Elijah already knew. Fully awake now, she yanked Elijah's half of the sheet away to cover herself.

"Hey!" He grabbed a pillow to cover his shivering loins.

On the riverbank, the cop made way for a pudgy older woman, dressed in a polka-dot housecoat and Sunday shoes.

Nana.

She glowered at Elijah, her big arms crossed against her bigger chest.

"We'd better go," Elijah said, but Annie was already bent over, hands in the water, paddling.

"I'm way ahead of you, pal."

The two coasted to shore. Big cop arms yanked them

one by one off the mattress and swaddled them in musty blankets from the trunks of their patrol cars. The cabin was a skeleton of what it once was. Charred pieces of framework reached crookedly toward the daytime sky. The barn was completely obliterated, reduced to a pile of planks and rubble. Trees were uprooted all around it.

Paramedics noted the gaping wound on Annie's shoulder. They were in the process of strapping her to a gurney when Elijah overheard the cops explain to Nana what *might* have happened: an old gas main blew, setting the cabin ablaze. In an amazing coincidence, an upstream dam broke and doused the fire, destroying the remains of the cabin and launching the two lovebirds into the lake.

Elijah didn't argue. It would only be a matter of time before the police would look for a different explanation after seeing the bullet holes, arrows and severed faces of his friends, but Elijah just wanted to survive the next minute — and the minute after it.

The paramedics wheeled Annie to the ambulance parked near the remains of the cabin. She wriggled one arm out of the white sheet that covered her and waved shyly at Elijah. He waved back.

"You never told me you had a girlfriend," Nana said, shaking her head.

Elijah watched the medics wrangle Annie into the back of the ambulance.

"Her name is Annie."

Surrounded by burly cops, he decided to go for broke. Maybe, if Nana exploded, one—or a dozen—of them might be able to hold her back.

"She's Wiccan."

After an awkward pause during which Elijah was unable to breathe, Nana shrugged. "At least she's religious."

Elijah exhaled. Crisis averted. His voice was hoarse from smoke inhalation but he continued. "Nana, I know what I did was wrong. I lied to you. I took advantage of your trust and I'm sorry for it, Nana, I am, but I have to know… *what is this place?*"

Elijah saw Nana had tears in her eyes. Actual tears.

"This was my father's place."

Elijah nearly fell over in shock. "*WHAT!*"

Nana, unconcerned, rummaged in her purse as she explained. "He was a man of God. He claimed the Lord visited him and told him the next child conceived here would be the Devil's child."

Elijah nodded. He knew *that* much.

"When he told his followers, they laughed at him and…" Her voice choked back emotion. "Those he didn't poison, he hacked to death with an axe. I hid in the woods. I was seven years old."

In an instant Elijah saw his grandmother anew. He had never once guessed she may have had suffering or tragedy in her life comparable to his. But then, he had never asked.

Nana removed her tissue bag. "Years later, after I had your father, I went back to the mountain and bought the property. I would never let this place out of my hands if I could help it and I would never tell anybody about what had happened."

"Why keep it secret? Why didn't you tell anybody?"

"Because... I *believed* him."

Elijah's jaw dropped. "But he was a murderer! He was crazy! How can you say you believed him?"

"Of course he was crazy, Elijah. Don't you think I knew that? But... he must have had his reasons."

She blew her nose heartily.

Movement caught Elijah's eye as he looked toward the barn. Several burly officers lifted a section of the roof away. Beneath it, causing several cops to gag, was George's lifeless body, still clutching his guts atop a pile of skeletons—the remains of Reverend Bob's congregation.

The police officers each turned in their direction. A few had their hands on their guns.

Elijah spun back to Nana, time running out, still trying to wrap his head around what she was saying. "Let me understand: you believe God visited your father, warned him not have anyone have sex under a full moon, then sat back and allowed him to murder everyone in his flock— including himself—all because they wouldn't believe him?"

"It was God's will."

Elijah was jumping up and down; he couldn't stand still and believe what his grandmother was saying. Not after what he'd been through the previous evening. Not after what Annie had showed him. "But that's not the God I choose to believe in!"

Nana began to cackle. "*Choose*? Ha! You don't get to choose! There is only *one* God…"

"Ma'am," the chief officer behind her spoke, "we need to ask you a few questions downtown."

They were surrounded by the entire police force.

Nana looked at Elijah one last time; her eyes were red but they still held their unflappable conviction.

He noted they were her father's eyes.

"Elijah, I forgive you, but if you *did* have sex up here… I pray it was safe sex." The police led her in the direction of their cars.

An image flashed in Elijah's head: he was on top of Annie in Nana's old bed. The image shifted to George handing him the green condom, then to Annie biting his nipple, to putting himself inside of Annie—

Oh, crap.

Across a flapping yellow line constructed of obligatory crime scene tape, a young reporter with frosty blond hair recorded a news report.

"Here, at what remains of the crime scene, four teens are dead in a scene that looks like it was out of a horror movie—"

Nana, overhearing this, broke from the officers and interrupted the reporter. "You call them horror movies. I call them Christian..."

The young blonde raked a hand in front of her throat, signaling to her cameraman to cut.

Clutching his blanket, Elijah ran over to the ambulance to check on Annie. The back doors were still open as the EMTs conferred and checked their logs. She sat up, holding her stomach. Her face, already in shock, found Elijah's.

"What is it?" he asked, inching forward.

The sheet that had once lain flat and white was now swollen and red. Blood seeped between her legs.

Before one of the attendants returned and shut the door, Annie called out to him, "It's kicking, Elijah! I can feel it kick!"

The door shut and the ambulance drove off, navigating its way through parked police cars and body bags, as it began the slow, precarious trip down the mountain path. Elijah could still hear Annie's muffled screaming as they drove off.

"It's kicking!"

He had chosen to believe in a different god, but in the end, there was only one. The same severe Old Testament God Nana had taught him all his years.

The one who loved horror movies.

And now he was in one.

No, God...

Nana stared into the camera lens, voice insistent, eager to be heard, as she clutched the reporter's microphone.

No, God, please...!

"Sinners sin. Get punished. God reigns."

No God! Please no!!! Noooooooooo...

Cue credits.

ABOUT THE AUTHOR

ERNIE VECCHIONE is an award-winning screenwriter, producer and novelist. He wrote and produced the Streamy and Webby nominated series SEX ED: THE SERIES, which has more than 160 million views worldwide. He has written for HBO and Miramax and is a winner of the Set In Philadelphia Screenwriting Competition.

You can learn more about Ernie and his upcoming projects on Facebook at www.Facebook.com/ErnieWriter, on Instagram at www.Instagram.com/ErnieWriter, or you can read his blog at www.ErnieBlog.com.